....

She actually swayed when he came into the room. He was wearing jeans and a pale blue polo shirt. His federal identification badge hung from one of his belt loops. He looked exactly as she remembered, tall and distractingly handsome.

"Shelby," he said softly as his hands gripped the bared flesh of her upper arms and his eyes bored into hers. "You have a son?"

Shelby nodded, then lowered her eyes. *Why was he here? Who decided to bring Dylan into this? She couldn't deal with him now. Her baby had to be her only concern.*

"Any idea why the police would think I might know something about the kidnapping?" Dylan asked.

Shelby felt his eyes on her and she held her breath. *Would he put it all together? How long would it take for him to realize the obvious?*

Dear Reader,

Welcome to THE ROSE TATTOO! More than food and drink are served up in this friendly neighborhood bar/restaurant in historic Charleston, South Carolina. There's a double dose of danger and desire on the menu, as well.

Kelsey Roberts, whose first Intrigue back in 1993 made her a nominee for Best New Writer, brings her deft touch for mystery and romance to this suspenseful miniseries.

At The Rose Tattoo, you will meet proprietor Rose Porter and all staff and patrons who somehow find danger...*and* the romance of a lifetime!

Look for the future titles in this series and become a regular at The Rose Tatoo!

Sincerely,

Debra Matteucci
Senior Editor and Editorial Coodinator
Harlequin Books
300 East 42nd Street
New York, New York 10017

Unspoken Confessions

Kelsey Roberts

Harlequin Books

TORONTO • NEW YORK • LONDON
AMSTERDAM • PARIS • SYDNEY • HAMBURG
STOCKHOLM • ATHENS • TOKYO • MILAN
MADRID • WARSAW • BUDAPEST • AUCKLAND

For Bonnie and Debra, who believed.

I would like to gratefully acknowledge the assistance of Pat Harding, Kay Manning and Carol Keane of Charleston, South Carolina: my crack research team.

ISBN 0-373-22326-9

UNSPOKEN CONFESSIONS

Copyright © 1995 by Rhonda Harding Pollero

THE ROSE TATTOO

Upper Level

Office

Closet

Office

Hall

Storage

L | M

Lower Level

Kitchen

Fireplace

Bar

L | M

CAST OF CHARACTERS

Shelby Hunnicutt—How could she tell Dylan that the kidnapped child they were seeking was his?

Dylan Tanner—He had put Shelby in the past, until a kidnapper pulled him into her present.

Jay Williams—The consummate law-enforcement official; he was revered and respected, even though he was sometimes blinded by his desire to make an arrest.

Rose Porter—Her past was as colorful as her name.

Ned Nichols—Was he using Chad to ensure Shelby's silence?

Keith Jackson—Shelby was his obsession. How far would he go to get her attention?

Victoria Conway—She's a great employee—punctual, professional...and a liar.

Chad Hunnicutt—He needs his mother.

Chapter One

"Have you called the police?"

Shelby nodded as she gulped in air. "They're on their way."

"Where's Cindy?" Rose asked, placing her hands on Shelby's trembling arms.

"I think she went into the kitchen," she answered. "As soon as I realized the baby was gone, I really lit into her."

"I should hope so! What was she doing? How did they get in?" Rose thundered.

Shelby glanced over her shoulder and saw the teenager hunched over the kitchen table. The muffled sounds of her crying filtered into the living room.

"She put him to bed around nine. She said she never heard so much as a peep."

"Peep, my foot!" Rose huffed. "You mean to tell me someone waltzes in here and snatches our baby, and *that* one didn't even feel a draft from the door?" She waved her thumb in the direction of the girl.

"The window was open when I went in to kiss him goodnight." The memory of that horrible moment brought with it a renewed flood of warm tears for Shelby. All at once, her mind filled with so many possibilities—none of them good. "What am I going to do?" she managed to choke out.

"I don't know," Rose answered with her usual candor.

The police arrived then. A virtual army of men and women, in all ranks, shapes and sizes. Rose brought one of them over to Shelby, who stood next to the window, peering out at the bustle of activity. She couldn't stand the thought of Chad being out there. With God only knew what kind of stranger.

"I'm Detective Greer, Mrs. Hunnicutt."

"Shelby," she said automatically.

"Shelby," he repeated in a soothing voice. "I need to get some information from you as soon as possible."

"Anything," she told him.

He smiled wanly and touched her elbow, directing her to the table in the center of the room. He reached into his pocket and pulled out a small notebook. As he flipped it open, he pushed the vase of cut flowers on the table off to one side.

She was only vaguely aware of what was happening in her own home. Rose was on the sofa, talking to one of the female officers. There was a man in the kitchen with Cindy. Still others moved past her toward the stairs, stopping only long enough to ask about the rooms on the second floor.

She tasted the remnants of salty tears as she moistened her lower lip.

"The FBI will be here soon, so I'll need to get some background."

"Chad is nine months old. He weighs twenty-two pounds and has some dark hair just beginning to grow. His eyes are blue, but not the same color as mine. He—"

"We'll get a recent picture," Greer said gently, interrupting her.

She nodded and said, "I just had some done at the mall. I'll get them."

"No." Greer placed his hands over hers. "Just tell me where they are."

"On the kitchen counter," she said.

"Do you live here alone?" he asked.

"Yes."

"And your husband?"

"I'm not married."

"Then the baby's father?"

"Isn't involved."

One of the detective's brows arched in an unspoken question.

"He isn't," she insisted.

"Give me his name and address," he stated as he poised his pen above the page.

She looked around then. There were at least a dozen people in the house. Judging from the beams of bright light flickering in the window, several officers were positioned outside, as well.

"His father couldn't have had anything to do with this," she insisted.

"We won't know until we talk to him," Greer pointed out.

"It isn't like that," she said. "Chad's father doesn't even know about him. I left without ever telling him I was pregnant."

The detective leaned back in the seat. His head tilted to one side as he regarded her for several long seconds. "If you're keeping information from us..."

"I wouldn't do that! My son is gone!"

"Will you at least tell me the guy's name?"

"I—"

A young uniformed officer came over and whispered something to Greer. He then placed a small plastic pouch in the detective's hand before retreating back out the front door.

"Do you recognize this?"

She reached out and took the bag. Inside was a small, round silver medallion on a broken chain. Instantly, she remembered. . . .

"This is very nice," she murmured.

She could smell the faint traces of his cologne. The medallion was between his thumb and forefinger. Her eyes remained transfixed as she watched him absently run the silver object along its chain.

She sensed the change in him. The knowledge brought with it a flood of anticipation that swirled in her stomach. Her nerves were electrified; her awareness was acute. All these weeks of waiting, wondering, dreaming, seemed near an end.

"What are you doing?" she asked through a smile when he moved around behind her.

"Protecting you," he murmured against her neck. His hands wound around her waist, his large fingers splayed against her abdomen.

"Is this part of your job description, Dylan?"

Her fingers laced with his.

"I know someone who wears one like this. His name is Dylan Tanner. He's an agent with Alcohol, Tobacco and Firearms. But I haven't seen him for a long time," Shelby finally answered. She retained her hold on the medallion, remembering all too vividly what it had looked like nestled in the dark mat of hair on Dylan's chest.

"Is this Tanner guy the baby's father?" Greer asked pointedly.

Shelby's only response was a faraway look that seemed to quiet the detective's inquiry—at least for the present. The front door burst open, and Helen Hopewell was ushered in by a pair of officers. Cindy, her eyes rimmed by damp red circles, went running to her.

Helen clutched the girl, but she was looking at Shelby. "I don't know what to say," Helen began, her expression pained.

"I never heard a sound!" Cindy wailed, and then dissolved into another fit of loud sobs.

Helen explained to Greer that she was the sitter's mother, and that she lived in the house three doors down the street. The officer who had been talking to Cindy was furiously scribbling notes as she spoke.

Greer motioned to one of the officers, whispered a directive, then dismissed him. Shelby watched him leave, the shock of what had happened to her baby slowly evolving into a sort of numbness tinged with a certain amount of denial. The room was filled with the telltale scent of baby powder, and other small reminders of Chad. Part of her mind insisted on believing that this was all some sort of nightmare. Eventually she would wake up, and he would be there, smiling, drooling, even crying.

Sometime later, an officer poked his head in the front door and said, "He's here."

"Chad!" she screamed, looking in the direction of her front door. A flood of bright lights projected the long shadow of a man.

"Is it Chad?" she asked anxiously as she jumped to her feet.

Rose, who had been standing with her supportively, shoved one of the officers to one side to allow Shelby a unobstructed view of the door.

"I'm sorry, Shelby," Greer said.

She actually swayed when he came into the room. He was wearing jeans and a pale blue polo shirt. His federal identification badge hung from one of his belt loops. He looked exactly as she remembered, tall and distractingly handsome. He walked with such arrogant authority that he was able to reach her in two long strides.

"Shelby," he said softly as his hands gripped the bared flesh of her upper arms.

"I'm Detective Greer, Agent Tanner," the smaller man asserted as he thrust his hand forward.

Dylan didn't take the hand, but simply said, "Greer." His eyes were trained on her. "You have a son?" Dylan asked.

Shelby nodded, then lowered her eyes. Why was he here? Who had decided to bring Dylan into this? She couldn't deal with him now. Chad had to be her only concern.

"Do you recognize this?" Greer asked as he passed the bagged medallion to Dylan.

He turned away from her and accepted the item. His dark brows drew together as he turned the bag over in his palm.

"I did have one like this. I lost it about six months back," he told the detective. "It does look like mine."

Greer nodded and took back the evidence bag. "We found it in the bushes below the nursery. Can you think of any way it could have gotten here?"

"You thought I might have had something to do with this?" Dylan asked Shelby.

She was standing so close that he could smell the faint scent of her perfume. But it wasn't like the last time they'd been together, he thought as his hands balled into fists. Her contagious smile was gone, replaced by a tormented expression clouding her blue eyes. The hair framing her face was as dark as his own, but unlike his, it fell in soft waves to her slender shoulders. Even in grief, Shelby was beautiful.

Rose piped up. "Of course she doesn't."

"Who are you?" Dylan countered, bracing his feet as he crossed his forearms over his chest.

"Rose Porter," the woman responded. "I'm Shelby's business partner."

Dylan turned away from Rose's narrowed green eyes and gave his full attention to Shelby. "Business partner? So you did break with Nichols?"

"He bought me out," she answered, moving fractionally closer to Rose as he watched her.

"Hey, Greer!" Rose bellowed. "Are you still in charge here? Or have you decided to let this guy run your investigation?"

The police official bristled at Rose's decidedly sarcastic tone. "What is it you'd like me to do?" Greer retorted.

"Find the kid," Rose volleyed back.

"That's what we're trying to do," he said defensively. "That's why I sent a car for Mr. Tanner."

"You're wasting time and resources," Shelby insisted. "You heard Dylan. He didn't even know I had a son."

"No," Dylan agreed quietly. "I didn't."

Shelby felt his eyes on her, and she held her breath. *Would he put it all together? How long would it take for him to realize the obvious?*

"Have you wasted the last couple of hours tracking him down instead of looking for Chad?" Rose demanded. Her arms flailed at her sides, dislodging her animal-print blouse from the thick black patent-leather belt cinching her waist.

Her loud, distinctive voice garnered the attention of the officers and technicians. Greer blanched, and a red stain seeped up from the neck of his rumpled white shirt.

"I'm following up on the only lead we've got. That's how we do things, Mrs. Porter. We look at every detail."

A flash of something passed between the two of them that Shelby wasn't able to decipher. While she considered Rose her dearest friend, she also recognized that her outspoken tendencies didn't always endear the raucous woman to strangers.

"What leads *have* you got?" Dylan asked the other officer.

Greer shrugged and said, "The neighbor across the street thinks he may have seen a strange car parked up the street. We're showing him catalogs now, to see if he can come up with a make or model year."

"Have your men checked out Nichols?" Dylan barked.

"Nichols?" Greer repeated.

Dylan turned to Shelby again, and his eyes bored into her. "Ned's the father, right?"

Shelby shifted her weight from foot to foot. She wanted to scream the truth, but something told her now was neither the time nor the place. Her only answer was her silence. She couldn't lie to Dylan. Not directly, at least.

"Ned Nichols was her business partner. ATF's been investigating him on and off for almost two years," Dylan explained.

"Why the hell didn't you tell me this?" Greer bellowed at Shelby.

She started at the harsh question, and was grateful for Rose's hand on her shoulder. "I haven't seen or spoken to Ned in more than a year," she answered stiffly, careful to keep her eyes averted and fixed squarely on one of Chad's stuffed elephants.

"Where can we find him?"

Shelby hesitated, then said, "Ned could not possibly be involved in this."

"He's slime," Dylan countered. "If you think being the kid's father would make a difference to a guy like Nichols, you're dead wrong, Shelby. Christ," he muttered. "The guy's old enough to be *your* father."

"Where can we find this Nichols?" Greer asked.

"Charleston Import Company," Dylan supplied, then rattled off the address.

Greer took the information and moved away.

"Would you mind leaving us alone for a minute?" Dylan asked Rose.

Shelby could sense her friend's misgivings. "It's okay, Rose," she said.

"Chad means everything to Shelby," Rose warned Dylan before she turned toward the kitchen.

The scent of coffee lingered in the air between them. Her entire body tensed under his close scrutiny. At any second she expected the light to dawn. *What then?* her mind screamed.

"You look tired," he said, guiding her to the chair. "Do you want to go up and lie down for a while?"

"I couldn't," she insisted. "The FBI told me that kidnappers usually make a ransom demand in the first few hours."

"I'm sure they'll find him, Shelby."

"He's only a baby!" she cried in a choking voice. "What if he's hurt? What if—"

"Don't do this to yourself," he said soothingly, kneeling in front of her. His square-tipped fingers rested on top of her knees. "I'm sure they'll have him back here before morning."

She looked into his eyes, hoping to draw on his confidence. His angled features were set in what she suspected was an artificially optimistic expression.

"Ned wouldn't take Chad," she told him.

Dylan's handsome features immediately hardened. "I know you've always wanted to believe the best about that guy, but—"

"He doesn't even know about the baby," she admitted, carefully watching for his reaction.

It wasn't good.

"You mean to tell me you never told the man he had a son?" Dylan demanded in a harsh whisper.

"I didn't tell Ned about the baby," she stated simply, feeling her face warm under the weight of her evasiveness.

"I thought the way you dumped me was cold," he observed. "I never would have thought you were capable of doing something this dishonest."

"My son is missing, Dylan! The last thing I need from you is a lecture on my decision making. You don't have the first clue what you're talking about. And besides, this doesn't really concern you."

"What is going on here?" Rose asked, in time with the rhythm of her spiked heels hitting the floor.

"Nothing," Shelby answered quickly.

"Well, it doesn't look like nothing," Rose muttered. "Just what did you say to her?" she asked Dylan. "Her hands are shaking, and she's crying again."

"Sorry," Dylan mumbled.

"I'm sorry your mother didn't eat you when you were born," Rose spit at him. Placing her hands on her rounded hips, she arched one neatly plucked brow toward the pile of coiffed blond hair that added height to her small frame.

"Look, lady," Dylan said, rising slowly, "I didn't mean to upset her."

"You did," Rose told him pointedly.

If his size intimidated her, nothing in her expression gave it away. Rose simply squared her shoulders and offered him one of her wilting looks. Shelby had seen it work magic on the most unruly patron. It didn't seem to be having much of an effect on Dylan.

"I really am sorry, Shelby," he said to her. "I was way out of line."

"Forget it," she breathed as she picked up one of the dozens of photos strewn across the table. A lump formed in her throat the instant she looked at the big eyes smiling back at her from the picture. They were nearly the same shade of electric blue-gray as those of the man standing just a few inches away. She felt the wetness of tears that flowed soundlessly.

"They'll find him, Shelby honey," Rose said. "You gotta have faith."

"I do," she lied. What she had was a deep, consuming pain in her chest. It was hard to keep her mind from wandering into those unspeakable places. Hard to keep her imagination from producing horrible scenarios.

"I know most of these guys, Shelby," Dylan said as he again knelt in front of her. "They'll find your little boy."

She nodded, afraid to speak, for fear of what she might say.

She lifted her head when she heard her front door open. One of the plainclothesmen walked in and whispered something to Greer. The detective's head moved fractionally, and it appeared to her that his guarded expression lightened just a bit.

Dylan rose and placed a hand on her shoulder as Greer
strode over.

"I don't want to get your hopes up..." he began.

"What?"

"Ned Nichols isn't at his house *or* his business. One of
his neighbors saw him leave his house around midnight."

Shelby held her breath and swallowed.

Greer continued, "He was carrying something wrapped
in a blanket."

Chapter Two

Dylan watched as her mouth dropped open. He should have expected it. Shelby had a definite blind spot where Nichols was concerned.

His gut knotted, and he rammed his fists in his pockets. She looked so shocked and scared that it took every ounce of his self-control for him to keep a level head. How could Nichols do this to her? How could *she* have had his son?

He looked away then. The thought of Shelby and Nichols together still rankled. More than it should. But it was because he remembered....

HIS LIPS BRUSHED against the sensitive skin just below her earlobe. The silky feel of her skin drew his stomach into a knot of anticipation. His grip tightened as his tongue traced a path up to her ear. He heard her breath catch when he teasingly nibbled the edge of her lobe.

His hands traveled upward and rested against her rib cage. He felt her swallow, heard the moan rumbling in her throat.

"You smell wonderful," he said against her heated skin.

"Dylan..." She whispered his name. "I don't think this is such a good idea."

His mouth stilled, and he gripped her waist, turning her in his arms.

"I've kept my hands off you for five weeks," he said. He applied pressure to the middle of her back, urging her closer to him.

"I know," she managed to say above her rapid heart-beat.

"I've never done this," he said.

Shelby's eyes flew open wider, and her expression registered obvious shock.

His chuckle was deep.

"I mean, I've done this," he went on. "I've just never been so attracted to a woman that I've been willing to compromise my professional responsibilities."

"Will this affect your job?"

"I hope so," he said as he claimed her mouth. The kiss lasted for several heavenly moments. "I just wouldn't want you to think I make a habit of this sort of thing."

"I don't think I am thinking," she admitted as she rested her cheek against his chest.

"I CAN'T BELIEVE Ned would take Chad," she finally said in a soft voice. "There's no reason for him to want to hurt either one of us."

Dylan snorted. "I can think of one." Turning to Greer, he continued, "Nichols knows that Shelby can put him away."

"But he's known that for more than a year!"

Dylan ignored the conviction in her tone. "For the past six months, I've been working it from the other end. My agency has reliable information that another shipment is due any day. Nichols's suppliers are about to make their move."

"Back up," Greer told him. "Shipment of what?"

"MAC-10s," he answered. "A large shipment of those guns, along with a hefty amount of ammunition, was stolen from an Israeli depot last month."

Greer let out a low whistle. "I guess it's too much to hope that you guys had him under surveillance?"

Dylan shrugged. "I've been working with a contact at the port, but I can call my superior."

"I'll keep my fingers crossed," Greer said.

"I still can't believe that Ned would be involved," Shelby said, wrapping several strands of her deep ebony hair around one finger.

Dylan remembered all too vividly how soft her hair was. How it had felt fanned out across his chest.

Shaking his head, he told himself he needed a breather. He was no good to Shelby when he couldn't stay focused. The kitchen offered the safe haven he needed. *What kind of man was he?* he wondered as he lifted the telephone receiver and dialed. Her kid was missing, and all he could think about was the memory of that one night.

A groggy male voice answered on the third ring. "Yeah?"

"Jay, it's Dylan. We've got a serious problem."

In the other room, Shelby was quickly losing hope. It had been nearly five hours. "Where could he be?" she asked.

"I know they'll find him," Rose answered. "And when they do, I'll arrange for a little justice for the dirtball that's responsible. Southern-style."

"That kind of talk won't help," Greer cautioned.

She watched as Rose leveled the man a pointed stare. While her partner was a small woman, Rose was an imposing person, with an impressive vocabulary of fierce looks.

"Well, what are *you* guys doing?" Rose demanded of the officer.

"We're following leads, Mrs. Porter," Greer answered. Then, rather ominously, he added, "All of them."

"Right," Rose muttered derisively.

Greer excused himself and wandered over to a small collection of men huddled in the corner of the living room. Some were busy connecting some sort of reel-to-reel tape machine to the telephone outlet. Others were occupied covering every inch of the room in a bluish black dust.

"We'll need your prints," a woman announced to Shelby as she placed what looked like a tackle box in the center of the table.

"What for?" Rose asked.

Shelby merely blinked.

"We need to print everyone who has had access to the house. Then we can eliminate friends and family when we begin to run comparisons."

"Why don't I go back to the Tattoo and bring whatever desserts are left for these folks?" Rose suggested.

Shelby felt her mouth drop open at the uncharacteristic suggestion. Not that Rose wasn't kind—she was. But she wasn't normally given to attacks of hostessing. Maybe she needed some way to deal with her emotions, Shelby speculated. Rose was definitely nervous. Perhaps a trip to their restaurant would do her some good.

"You can do my prints when I get back," Rose told the technician.

The uniformed woman simply shrugged as she began taking ink pads and file cards from inside the tackle box. "Give me your left hand first," she instructed Shelby.

Numbly Shelby complied, her eyes searching for Dylan. She found him in the kitchen, talking on the telephone. His eyes, which were neither gray nor blue, but a devastating combination of the two, were thickly lashed and hooded. A lock of his jet black hair had fallen forward to rest just above his brows. His chiseled mouth was pulled into a tight line.

"Give me your right hand now, please."

"Sorry," Shelby mumbled, starting. The woman looked down at her with compassion, and that was almost enough of a catalyst to set her tears off yet again.

Crying wouldn't help. She could cry later, once Chad was home.

Cindy was fingerprinted next, and then allowed to leave in the comfort of her mother's supportive arms. Shelby felt a pang of envy, followed by a dose of anger. Intellectually she knew she shouldn't blame the sitter, but she needed a hate object until the kidnapper was found.

"No," she whispered as her head dropped forward. "I need Chad."

"We'll find him," Dylan said.

She looked up at him through her unshed tears. "Why haven't I been contacted?"

He shrugged his broad shoulders. "The ball's in his court. You've just go to keep it together until Ned decides the time is right."

"It still doesn't make sense to me. Ned has no reason to take my son."

"His son, too," Dylan countered. "You know," he began as he slid into the seat next to her, "maybe that's the reason."

"What?"

"Maybe Nichols found out he had a son and just decided to make himself the custodial parent."

"That isn't possible," she told him.

"Why not? I'll admit I had a similar thought when the officer showed up at my house tonight."

"What thought?" she asked, in a barely audible tone.

"Before he told me how old your son was, I wondered if I was..."

"Chad is nine months old," she asserted.

"I know. And I can add and subtract."

"Your math skills aren't going to bring my son back," she pointed out stiffly.

"Did you know you were pregnant when we were together?"

"Dylan," she began as she rose, "I don't want to get into all this with you. Not now."

"You're right," he said quickly. "I'm sorry."

Greer came over then. His forehead was wrinkled into a series of deep lines. He spoke to Dylan first. "Did you get in touch with Special Agent Williams?"

"He's on his way."

"Your boss is coming here?" Shelby interjected.

His dark head dipped slightly. "He's alerting the unit."

"But I thought the FBI was in charge of handling kidnappings."

"Jay spoke to them and offered to spearhead things because we already have so many agents in place."

"In place where?" she asked.

"We've got agents undercover at the import company. People already on the inside of Ned's organization. We've got wiretaps, some surveillance, the whole nine yards. It would be a waste for the FBI to duplicate everything we've done."

The creases in Greer's forehead became shallower. "I think you're lucky in this respect, Shelby. Having Alcohol, Tobacco and Firearms in on this will save time. Time is important when you've got a missing kid."

The phrase *missing child* conjured up all sorts of unpleasant images in her brain. Milk cartons and posters. Billboards and grim news footage. She swayed.

Dylan's hands went to her shoulders, steadying her.

"Are you sure you don't want to lie down for a bit?"

"I'm sure," she answered.

"Actually," Greer began, "there's something I'd like you to consider."

Shelby's eyes flew to his face. "What?"

"The morning news shows start in about forty-five minutes. I'd like you to think about making an appeal for Chad in front of the cameras."

"Go on TV?"

Greer nodded.

"The exposure might do some good," Dylan suggested.

His hand touched her shoulder as she looked from man to man. "Will it help?"

"It'll get his face out there. It will make it hard for the kidnapper to hide him if the whole city of Charleston is looking for him."

"I don't think I can do it," she said, in a quavering voice.

"Sure you can," Dylan insisted with a weak smile.

"I'll be there with you," Greer offered.

"So will I," Dylan added.

"No," Greer said, with a slight shake of his head. "If it is Nichols, seeing you might not sit too well."

She saw the reluctance in Dylan's eyes. She felt an unexpected flash of disappointment. *What is wrong with me?* her brain screamed. *I need to get him away from here!* Letting him see pictures of Chad was one thing. But how could she keep her secret if Dylan saw her little boy up close? Surely he'd discover her deception.

"Greer is right." She looked directly into Dylan's arresting eyes. "In fact, there's no reason for you to even stay here."

She saw him flinch.

"I want to stay here until I find out why my medallion, if it is mine, was found here."

"It couldn't be yours," she argued. "You said yourself that you lost yours a long time ago."

"It isn't exactly a one-of-a-kind item," Greer pointed out.

"Right. See?" Tension stretched between her and the tall man.

"No," Dylan answered firmly. "I don't see."

"We're getting off track," Greer said. "Are you willing to go on camera?" he asked Shelby.

"If you think it will help find Chad."

"Good," he said with a nod. "I'll set it up."

When Greer went to the front door, he was greeted by Rose, her arms weighted down by a large box filled with foil-wrapped packages.

"I brought everything I could think of," she said as she placed the box on the edge of the table and slid it toward the center. "Keith left the kitchen in a mess. Remind me to give him hell when this is all over."

"Who is Keith?" Dylan asked.

Rose unpacked items as she spoke. "He's our cook. No," she added with a smirk, "he's our chef. He gives me one of those snotty looks if I call him a cook."

Greer and several of the other officers came over to the table. Shelby stepped back, nearly sickened by the smell of the food. Dylan moved with her.

"Does Keith always leave your kitchen a mess?" he asked.

"Not usually," Shelby responded, without really giving the matter much thought. "He's a character. Rose isn't fond of him, because she thinks he puts on airs."

"And what do you think?"

"I think he's trying to overcome his past."

"His past?"

"Keith learned to cook in Europe."

"That's impressive."

"He learned to cook on army bases in Europe."

"Oh."

"Rose doesn't much like airs. It has something to do with her marriage."

"She's married?"

"Was," Shelby said. "She rarely talks about it, and I learned early on not to ask."

"Aren't the two of you friends, as well as partners?"

"We're very good friends." She glanced up at him, meeting his gaze directly. "Part of being friends is respecting each other's privacy."

"Nice to see you're still willing to turn a blind eye where your friends are concerned."

"Don't start with me, Dylan," she warned him. "I'm worried sick about my son, and I certainly don't intend on allowing you to take potshots at me now."

"Shelby," he said, gripping her upper arm, "I'm sorry. Really. I don't know what possessed me to say something so stupid."

She waffled as her emotions warred with her common sense. Now would be the perfect time to tell him to take a hike. *So why don't I?* she wondered.

"Forget it," she managed.

The grip on her arm loosened. "I'm not going anywhere, Shelby."

"But there's really nothing—"

"Shelby, honey, eat something," Rose said as she passed a croissant forward.

"I can't."

"You've got to try," Rose insisted. "You aren't going to do the baby any good if you starve yourself."

"Maybe later," she said, offering her friend a forced smile.

"It's already morning." Rose inclined her head in the direction of the window.

"Maybe coffee," Shelby suggested, and she infused lightness into her voice.

"You won't have time for coffee," Greer said as he joined them. "The television people are all set up. They're waiting for you outside right now."

"What do I do?" Shelby asked the officer.

"We've given them a picture of Chad that they'll show when the piece airs. All you need to do is ask for the safe return of your son."

"Then what?"

"Then we wait," Dylan answered.

The lights were hot. And they were so bright that she couldn't see beyond the porch. She knew there were people out there, because she could see several pairs of feet radiating out from under the harsh white glare. It took several protracted seconds for her eyes to adjust to the brilliant light.

"Miss Hunnicutt?" someone shouted. "Can you lift your chin a bit?" Then: "That's good. Look straight ahead, toward the red light."

She found the small glowing dot and stared at it until her tired eyes began to burn.

"Anytime you're ready," the faceless voice called.

"I . . . um . . . If you're listening to me, please bring my son back. I don't want to see you punished. If you're afraid of being caught, please take him to a hospital, or to a firehouse. He's all I have. Please, please, let him come home."

She was shaking by the time she went back inside the house. Rose immediately appeared at her side, as did Dylan.

"Do you think that will do any good?" she asked no one in particular.

"Of course it will," Rose said firmly. "If nothing else, Chad's face will be all over the morning news. He's bound to be noticed by someone. He's too cute to fade into the woodwork."

Shelby smiled then. "I hope so."

"Jay's here," Dylan noted, turning away from them.

She watched as the man entered the room. He was the type of person who naturally commanded attention. He had that air of authority, that stoic sort of focus, that Shelby had always found intimidating. Now, however, she found the determined set of his squared chin comforting. Jay Williams would be a definite asset in their hunt for Chad.

"Miss Hunnicutt," he said as he approached.

His nondescript dark brown suit matched his eyes and hair. In fact, everything about him was so neat and perfectly matched that Shelby had the keen sense that she was in the presence of a Ken doll. His shirt was straight and white, as were his teeth. His shoes were polished, their laces perfectly spaced and knotted, so that each lace ending precisely matched its twin.

"Agent Williams," she said by way of greeting.

"Miss Hunnicut. And you must be Rose Porter," he said to a visibly surprised Rose.

"That's right."

"You and Miss Hunnicutt own the Rose Tattoo, on East Bay?"

"Yep," Rose answered.

Shelby noticed a guarded look fall over her friend's face.

"Any other investors?"

The agent's attention was fully on Rose.

"No," Shelby answered.

"Is that right, Mrs. Porter?"

She watched as Rose looked down and then began to tap her thumbs against her thighs. "I'm the owner of record."

"Then you deny having any other investors?" Williams went on in a badgering tone.

"What is this—?" Shelby's words were cut off when Dylan reached out and gave her hand a pointed squeeze.

"I'm carrying a note," Rose said softly.

"With a bank?" Williams demanded.

Greer and one of the ATF agents appeared then, apparently drawn by the heated interrogation.

"Not with a bank. No."

Shelby looked at her friend. Rose refused to make eye contact with her.

"Do you know Mitch Fallon?"

"Mitch Fallon?" Shelby repeated. She recognized the name from various newspaper reports.

"I know Mitch," Rose reluctantly answered.

"Doesn't he hold your note?"

"I borrowed money from him."

"At twenty-five percent?" Williams hammered.

"Look." Rose's voice had risen an octave. "Mitch lent me money when the banks wouldn't touch me."

"He's what's commonly referred to as a loan shark, isn't he, Mrs. Porter?"

"I suppose."

"And he has a reputation for collecting interest in some rather violent ways, does he not?"

"He's never been anything but straight with me," Rose shot back.

"Everything on the up-and-up?" Williams asked.

"You bet."

"Never had any trouble from Fallon?"

"Never."

"Then he doesn't mind that you're three months behind on your payments?"

Chapter Three

"You owe money to a loan shark?" Shelby gasped.

"How do you think I kept the Tattoo going before you?" Rose countered in a subdued tone. "Mitch couldn't have anything to do with this, Shelby," she continued. "I know he's got a bad—"

"So you don't deny that you are indebted to Fallon?" Williams asked.

"Of course not," Rose shot back. "Mitch and I are old friends. He lent me money because of that. He knows Shelby and I have been spending a fortune trying to build the business. He agreed to let me slide for a while."

Agent Williams's face dissolved into an expression of guarded concentration as he listened to Rose's explanation. Shelby looked from Rose to Jay, then to Dylan.

He appeared to be mulling the revelation over. His eyes were clouded and unreadable. "When was the last time you talked to Fallon?" he asked.

Rose shrugged, then said, "Week ago. Maybe ten days."

"Check it out," Williams barked to one of the other officers gathered in the dining room. "Withholding information in a kidnapping is a serious offense," he warned Rose.

"I didn't withhold squat," she told the stiff man.

"Really?" he asked, in a tone Shelby thought sounded strangely like a taunt.

"Really."

"You'd better be telling me the truth, Mrs. Porter."

"And you'd better find the kid," Rose responded.

"This isn't getting us anywhere," Shelby said. "First you start screaming that it has to be Ned. Now you're leaning toward some loan-shark person I've never even met. Instead of attacking my friends and grabbing at straws, would you please do something constructive to find my son?"

"We are." Dylan spoke close to her ear. "I'm sure we'll have him back as soon as we find Nichols."

Pivoting on the ball of her foot, Shelby angled her body so that she faced Dylan. "Just humor me," she pleaded. "Don't waste all your energy and resources on Ned. I know he wouldn't take my baby."

"Then give me an alternative that makes sense," he said in a soft tone.

"How am I supposed to know?" she wailed. Her hands flew into the air, then slapped against her thighs before dangling helplessly at her sides.

"Other than Nichols, do you have any enemies? Anyone that would want to hurt you?"

She shook her head. "I don't have any enemies. Not even Ned."

He let it pass, even though it pained him to keep his thoughts on the subject to himself. She looked rough. There was strain around her eyes, in her voice. And it was getting to him.

"What about the bar?" his boss asked.

"Restaurant and bar," he heard Rose say.

"Whatever," Jay muttered.

Shelby hugged her arms against her body and let out a breath. It looked to him as if she was losing the battle to keep her tears at bay.

"We're just getting off the ground. We cater mostly to young professionals, but we get a few neighborhood folks," Shelby said.

"Employees?" Dylan asked.

"We gave all this to Greer!" Rose fairly shouted.

He saw the slight tremor in Shelby's hand when she touched her partner's forearm. He wanted to reach out to her, promise her everything would work out. Only he wasn't sure he believed it. Not when they had so little to go on. *And what?* he wondered for the umpteenth time, *was my medallion doing at her place?*

"Detective Greer will no longer be directly involved, so you'd better give it to me," he told Shelby. "ATF will be handling the investigation."

"There's Keith," she began. "He's the chef. Then we have Tory—Victoria Conway. She's a waitress and tends bar on and off. Josh Davis is our regular bartender. And Erica and Kelly wait tables."

"What about you?" Jay asked Rose.

"I own the place," she answered. Dylan noted that the Porter woman's spine had gone rod-straight but she still wasn't making eye contact with his boss. He decided to file that bit of information away for the time being.

"Do you work, as well?" Jay asked.

"We both do whatever is necessary, Agent Williams."

It was Shelby's soft voice, with its cultured Southern drawl, that answered the question.

Being from New York, Dylan often found the slow Southern way of speaking annoying. But not hers. Not Shelby's. The cadence of her speech wasn't slow, it was seductive.

"Something wrong?"

He was pulled back to the present by the sudden jab of Jay's elbow into his side.

"What?"

"Your expression," Jay said, prompting him. "Think of something?"

Dylan shook his head and said, "No."

"Shelby, honey," Rose said quietly, "go up and rest for a little while. I'll stay here."

"I can't."

"Sure you can," she insisted.

Shelby felt herself being pushed toward the stairs. "I need to be here in case—"

Rose cut in. "Don't be stupid. I'll be upstairs in a split second if anything happens. I promise."

"I'll walk you up."

Shelby froze at the base of the steps when she heard Dylan's offer. She couldn't very well insist that he stay away from her, not without a lot of explaining.

"That isn't necessary," she said, in a voice she hoped sounded aloof.

"I know it."

"Go on," Rose urged.

The handrail, which had been carved by a previous owner of the house, was covered in a thin film of blue fingerprint dust. But Shelby noticed only the marks on the walls. They weren't from the forensic team. They were small gouges and scratches from Chad's toys. She felt her chest fill with weighted guilt. How many times had she admonished him for scraping the wall with a toy? What she wouldn't give to have him home, crawling precariously up the stairs with a toy in each hand—that defiant smile on his round face.

Stopping at the top of the stairs, Shelby turned and looked into the shadowy room. She felt Dylan's fingers fan against her back as she reached for the wall switch.

Light flooded the small space. A clown smiled at her from above the crib, which had been pulled away from the wall and left at a strange angle. The window was covered with the blue dust, as was the top of the dresser. Only the neatly organized changing table appeared to have made it through the onslaught undisturbed.

"This doesn't seem real to me," she said in a near whisper.

"I can't imagine how you must feel."

She turned then, and lifted her chin in order to meet his gaze directly. "Numb."

She watched as his dark head lowered and he pressed his lips together.

"We'll find him," he told her as his fingertips found the underside of her chin.

"I hope you're right."

"Believe me."

"I have to," she said as she bowed away from his touch.

Flipping the switch, Shelby backed out of the room and headed down the narrow hallway toward her room. There, in the golden rays of the morning light, she saw it.

"What on earth?" she exclaimed. "What is that doing here?"

"Jay!" she heard Dylan call as she moved to the foot of her bed.

Resting just on the edge was an odd rectangular black item. She went to pick it up when Dylan's hand clamped over her wrist.

"Don't touch it!"

"But what if—"

Jay, with Greer on his heels, hurried into the room. Someone turned on the overhead lamp.

"What is it?"

"A videotape," Dylan answered.

"Is it yours?" Jay asked her.

"I don't think so," Shelby said after she looked on the side for a label. "No. It's not one of mine."

"Get the lab boys up here," Jay said.

Shelby looked down at her wrist, suddenly realizing that the warmth was from Dylan's viselike grip. His skin tone was darker than her own, despite the similar coloring of their hair and eyes. Using her free hand, she tapped the back of his hand with her fingers, without ever meeting his eyes or saying a word. She didn't dare let him know how his touch still affected her.

A small swarm of men crouched around the videotape, photographing, measuring, fingerprinting, mumbling. It felt as if hours had passed by the time they finally relented and allowed her to place the tape in the machine in her room.

Shelby and the others stood in a semicircle at the foot of her bed. She stared at the screen, watching as the static slowly organized itself into an image.

"Oh, God," she whispered through the fingers of her trembling hand.

"Is that him?" Dylan asked.

She nodded as she felt his fingers gently move to her waist. "That's the outfit I left for Cindy to put on Chad after she gave him his bath."

"Do you recognize anything else?" Jay asked. "Any of the surroundings?"

Shelby concentrated on the television screen. Chad was asleep on a small blanket, guarded by a collection of plush stuffed animals. When his small body moved involuntarily, a hand appeared in the frame.

"Looks like a woman," she heard someone remark.

"What's that?" Jay asked.

"Maybe a ring," Dylan answered.

The tape ran out then, leaving Shelby feeling shaken and more confused than ever.

"He looks like he's being well cared for," Dylan said against her ear.

"If you can call being kidnapped well cared for."

"Run the tape again," Jay told one of the officers as soon as it became apparent that there was nothing else on the video.

They stood in silence and watched the tape for a second, then a third time. She was surprised when her chest knotted with a sudden burst of anger. Who was the woman on the tape? And why had she taken Chad?

"See if you can get a blowup of the ring," Dylan said before the lab technicians spirited the tape away.

"And have the report sent directly to me," Jay added.

Shelby was left with only Dylan and the tall, slim Agent Williams in the room with her.

"Has anyone been around your restaurant lately? Anyone ask you about your son?"

Shelby shook her head. "No one."

"Is it common knowledge that you have a son?" Dylan asked.

"Yes," she answered defensively. Dylan was treading dangerously close to an area Shelby resented being questioned about. "I quite often take Chad to work with me."

"To a bar?"

She leveled Dylan an angry stare. "The Rose Tattoo is more than just a bar, Dylan. It's a restaurant, *and* my place of business. Stop saying it like you're implying I run some sleazy truck stop out along I-95."

"Okay," Dylan said, raising his hands in mock surrender. "I wasn't criticizing you."

"Not much," she muttered under her breath.

"Let's get back to the issue," Jay suggested.

Shelby guessed the man had picked up on the tension in the air. She wondered how long it would be before someone put it all together. *Then what?* her brain cried.

"What about at the market? Or shopping?" Jay continued. "Anybody approach you recently? Maybe say something about the baby."

"No," she said on an expelled breath. "Nothing like that has happened."

"Think, Shelby," Dylan urged, in a slightly raised voice. "Maybe someone commented on how cute he is? Something like that?"

Shrugging, she began to pace in the small area between the two men and the now silent television set. "I get compliments about him all the time. Chad's an adorable child."

She glanced at the two men and felt her face redden at the same time. Jay was stoic, but Dylan seemed to have allowed a small smile to penetrate his rigid facade.

"Maybe someone found him more adorable than normal?" The suggestion came from Jay.

"Nothing jumps out at me," she said. "I can't think of anything."

"Okay," Dylan said, shoving his hands into the front pockets of his jeans.

Shelby was distracted for a fraction of a second. For just that instant, she allowed her mind to fix on the outline of his well-muscled thighs. On the way the soft denim hugged his tapered hips.

"What about the woman on the tape?" Dylan continued. "Judging from the weathering of her skin, I'd say she was probably over fifty. Definitely spends time outdoors."

"Right," Jay agreed as he stroked an imaginary beard with his left hand. "We can assume she's local, since the tape showed up here so quickly."

"I don't see how she got it up here," Dylan added. "This place is crawling with cops."

"I think we can assume we're dealing with a very resourceful individual," Jay said.

"And it's not Ned," Shelby stated. Her remark was greeted with resistance from both men. Dylan's reaction seemed more pronounced than Jay's, but then, everything about Dylan left a strong impression on her.

"The tape doesn't exonerate Nichols," Jay said in a paternalistic tone.

"But we all agree that it was a woman's hand that pulled the blanket over Chad."

"Which simply could mean that Ned has an accomplice. Maybe she's the elusive ex-wife we were never able to track down."

She met Dylan's eyes and read the conviction there. "Dylan," she began reasonably, "isn't it possible that you are so convinced that Ned is evil that you're twisting things to make them fit?"

Dylan's dark head shook vigorously. "Hardly" was his derisive reply.

"He's right," Jay agreed. "It still appears as if Nichols is our best suspect."

"How can you say that?" Shelby asked. "There's nothing to indicate Ned is in any way involved in all this."

"Nothing except the fact that your son is gone," Dylan told her.

"A man, most likely Ned, has to be involved. I don't think a fifty-plus-year-old woman scaled the side of your house, not once, but twice," Jay told her. "Once to take the baby, and once to plant the tape."

"Why leave a tape?" Shelby asked. "Why would someone want to torment me like this?"

"Maybe it isn't to torment you," Jay suggested.

"Right," she heard Dylan say.

"I don't understand."

Dylan took two steps that brought him right in front of her. His breath washed over her face in warm waves. Shelby struggled with her strong urge to take a step backward.

"Maybe this is Nichols's way of letting you know Chad is all right."

"That's crazy!"

"Not necessarily," Jay said. "Nichols always did have a soft spot for you. And besides, since he's the baby's father, maybe in his sick little mind, he's trying to be humane."

Shelby sidestepped Dylan and turned toward the window. Wrapping her arms around herself, she tried to make some sense out of their farfetched assertions. "Ned would not do this to me," she breathed.

"He's an arms dealer, Shelby. Do you really think he's above kidnapping?"

She stiffened at Dylan's question. She had never wanted to believe that about Ned. He'd been good to her, and she owed him a debt of gratitude. But she and Dylan had been over this ground time and time again. She knew he would never understand her feelings, any more than she could understand his obsessive need to continue with the accusations.

"He wouldn't do this to me," she said again.

"How can you be so sure?" he thundered from behind her. "I know you don't want to accept that Ned is less than perfect, but be real, Shelby. The man finally realized you were a potential hazard. When he found out you'd had his kid, it was like playing right into his hands."

"You're reaching," she said, without turning toward him. She could almost feel his intense eyes boring into her back. She didn't dare risk facing him, not while Chad's parentage was being discussed.

"I'm not reaching, and you know it, Shelby." Her name came out as a husky whisper. "No one else has any reason to take your baby. Nichols has to be behind this."

"No. There has to be some other explanation," she said as she bowed her head.

She felt his hands move to her neck. He began a gentle kneading massage of the tense muscles between her shoulders. She was reminded of the magical way he had touched her. It seemed like a lifetime ago.

"Don't fight us on this," he said. "We aren't out to crucify Nichols. Jay and I only want to help you get your son back."

Shelby turned then, drawn by the soft invitation in his deep voice. She looked up at him through the veil of her thick lashes. "I'm not fighting you," she told him. "I just want to make sure that nothing goes unchecked. I'm just afraid that if Ned isn't guilty, we'll have wasted too much time and effort when—"

The shrill sound of the telephone split the air. Shelby jumped at the unexpected sound before brushing Dylan aside and running toward the nightstand.

When she reached the table, her hand seemed to freeze in midair, hovering just above the receiver.

"Pick it up," Dylan instructed.

Shelby looked to Jay, who gave a reassuring nod of his head.

With trembling fingers, she lifted the phone off the cradle and placed it at an angle near her ear. Dylan leaned against her, pressing his head next to hers.

"Hello?" she managed in a small voice.

There were some muffled sounds, followed by a raspy voice that said, "Cute kid. It'd be a shame if something was to happen to him."

Chapter Four

"Who is this?" she shouted into the receiver.

"Now, Shelby. If I told you my name, it would take all the fun out of it."

"Where's Chad? Is he all right?"

She heard the faint sound of cruel laughter. Her hand went up to brush the strands of her hair away from her eyes. Her heart pounded against her chest, making it nearly impossible for her to hear the muffled voice.

"He's fine. And he'll stay that way, as long as you do what I tell you."

"Anything," she promised. "Just don't hurt him."

"Shelby...Shelby... You've got to have some faith."

"Please let me talk to him. Hold the phone against his ear so that he can hear my voice—"

"There'll be time enough for that later," the voice said. "I'll be in touch."

"Wait! Please!" she yelled into the phone.

"He's gone," Dylan said. She could feel him move away from her. "It wasn't long enough for a trace."

She slammed the phone down with the full force of her frustration. Warm tears welled up in her eyes, but she refused to crumple. *Not yet,* she told herself.

"Was there anything familiar about the man?" Dylan asked.

"No," she answered softly. Shelby sat on the edge of the bed and cradled her head in her hands. She desperately wanted to scream.

"I'll go and check with the guys downstairs," Williams said. "Maybe they got lucky."

When she lifted her head, Shelby found Dylan staring down at her. His shoulders were slumped forward, and he appeared to share her dejected mood. The corners of his chiseled mouth moved slightly, lingering somewhere near an apology.

"He didn't ask for anything," she finally managed to say.

Dylan shrugged. "He could have been feeling you out. Or..."

"Or what?"

"Or—" Dylan shoved his hands into his pockets "—he could be fronting for someone else, who might make his demands known at a later date."

"I presume you're trying to tell me that you think the caller is somehow connected to Ned."

He nodded. "Nichols can't very well call. He knows you would recognize his voice."

"Why are you so convinced it's Ned?"

"Because nothing else makes sense," he told her. "Crimes are very rarely committed by strangers."

"Is that where we get the expression 'random act of violence'?" she shot back at him.

"I didn't say it doesn't happen," he stated reasonably. "I'm just trying to explain to you that it's rare."

"Why would anyone I know want to take my son?" she asked. "I'm hardly in a position to pay a sizable ransom. And I don't have any power. Nothing makes any sense."

"You have power over Nichols."

She looked at the ceiling and let her breath out slowly. "I explained the situation to you more than a year ago, Dylan. I never had any firsthand knowledge of Ned's dealings outside the import company."

"But you could have gotten it, if you'd continued to work with me."

"That wasn't an option," she said softly, careful to avoid his eyes.

"And I guess now I know why."

She watched in nervous silence as he began to pace back and forth. His muscular shoulders pressed against the fabric of his shirt with each intake of breath. Then his hand went up to rake through his thick mass of black hair, which he wore to a length just below his collar.

"I brought you up some herbal tea."

Shelby had been so busy studying Dylan's profile that she hadn't heard her friend come up the stairs. Rose expertly balanced the tray in one hand while she cleared a space on the nightstand with the other.

"You didn't have to do that," Shelby told her.

"You need to get some rest," Rose returned as she patted Shelby's hand. "There's nothing for you to do until that bozo calls back."

Rose's green eyes shimmered with a kindness at odds with the thick layers of makeup that were part of her image.

Shelby managed only a small smile in response.

"You," Rose said, turning in Dylan's direction, "go on downstairs and see if you can muzzle that boss of yours."

Dylan's expression lightened considerably. "I don't think Shelby should be alone."

"That's why I'm here, Sherlock. I'm the friend, you're the officer. The friend offers support and companionship. The cop investigates.'' Rose planted her hands firmly on her hips. ''Go down and see if you can discover if Williams is thinking with both lobes of his brain.''

''You shouldn't talk about Agent Williams like that,'' Shelby said as soon as Dylan had left the room, grumbling under his breath.

''He's not *doing* anything,'' Rose snorted as she began to pour tea from the small pot.

''They're convinced Ned has Chad.''

After filling the cup, Rose took a breath and patted her stiff blond curls into place. ''It's not really any of my business, but are you sure you're going about this the right way?''

Shelby felt her brows draw together. ''What do you mean?''

''Well,'' Rose said slowly, ''are you sure it's such a good idea to let Williams handle this, instead of Greer and the FBI?''

''No,'' Shelby answered quickly. ''But I'm not sure I have a choice. But I know Agent Williams is a very capable, driven individual.''

''How do you know him?''

Shelby smiled then. ''Wait a minute. Doesn't this violate our 'don't ask about the past' agreement?''

''That was before Chad was kidnapped,'' Rose answered. ''You don't have to tell me anything,'' she continued. ''I just never figured you to have been involved with the cops, is all.''

''I wasn't involved,'' Shelby said. ''Not really, anyway.''

''That isn't how I see it.''

Shelby's head came up, and she met Rose's inquisitive stare.

"Look, Shelby," Rose began as she took a seat next to her on the bed. "I saw the way you reacted to Dylan Tanner. And while I have always thought Chad was the spitting image of you, after seeing—"

"Enough!" Shelby interjected. She didn't want Rose to say it aloud. "I think I'll take your advice and try to rest for a while."

Rose hesitated, and Shelby feared her friend might press the issue. But, Rose being Rose, she simply nodded and quietly left the room.

Shelby stared at the door long after it had closed. If Rose had figured it out, how long would it take Williams? Or, worse yet—Dylan?

"WAKE UP, Shelby."

She did more than wake up. Shelby leapt to her feet with her heart pounding. Dylan was next to the bed, his face a mixture of anticipation and anxiety.

"What is it?" she asked as she vigorously rubbed her hands over her burning eyes. "Have you found Chad?"

"You've got to get to your restaurant," he said, gently nudging her toward the door. "Keith called and said the kidnapper called you. He's going to call back in—" Dylan paused and checked his watch "—less than twenty minutes."

"Oh, Lord," she moaned as she hurried down the stairs.

Her living room was no longer a hub of activity. Williams and two other officers were seated by the reel-to-reel machine, their faces expressionless.

"We'll wait here," Williams said to her. "Dylan can take you over. Mrs. Porter is already there, waiting by the phone. She said she'd stall if the call comes before you get there."

Shelby noticed a strain in Williams's voice. She wondered if this development had ominous overtones that no one was willing to admit to.

"Keys?" Dylan asked, offering his palm.

Shelby had to think for several seconds before her dulled brain recalled where she had left her purse. Shaking away the few remnants of sleep, she grabbed her bag off the side table and pulled her key ring free from the pocket.

"I'll drive," Dylan said.

She squinted against the bright afternoon sunlight. The pleasant scent of the flowers seemed an unkind intrusion into her grim thoughts. She followed Dylan across the lawn, sidestepping gouges in the turf that she guessed had been left by the television crews early that morning.

"What's the fastest way?"

She gave him directions by rote, her mind still not fully functional. It wasn't the result of the fitful few hours of sleep she'd had. No, Shelby was distracted by the sight of her son's empty car seat. And the brightly colored plastic rings abandoned on the floorboards.

She shut her eyes and summoned strength from her dwindling reserves. "Why the restaurant?" she asked.

Dylan gripped the wheel tightly and said, "Maybe he knows we've got a trace on your home phone."

"Can't you put the same equipment at the Tattoo?"

She saw him shake his head.

"Not enough time. But Jay's making the necessary arrangements to have that taken care of ASAP."

"Drive around back," she said, pointing toward the alleyway next to the Rose Tattoo.

The scraping of the car's underside drew the attention of the few patrons scattered along the restaurant's porches. She could see their curious expressions as she looked past Dylan.

He brought the car to an abrupt halt between the building and Keith's black Chevy. Shelby quickly forced open the door and stepped onto the weathered stone drive. Her heels echoed in the cavernous space as she walked toward the back entrance.

Almost immediately, her senses were assaulted by a barrage of odors from the kitchen. Dylan was right behind her as she slipped past the bustle of the work area and headed up the back stairs.

She had to turn sideways in order to pass by the stacks of boxes lining the small hallway. She found Keith and Rose waiting in their office.

Keith was tall and slender, with straight blond hair that he shaved just above his ears. A cubic-zirconia stud sparkled in his left earlobe. It seemed an appropriate accessory for his starched white chef's ensemble.

As she entered, Keith pulled himself up to his feet, wiping his hands on the fronts of his trousers. His eyes fluttered from her face to an area near her feet.

"Has he called back?" Dylan asked.

"Not yet," Rose answered. Then she turned to the chef and said, "You go on back downstairs. Take care of anything that comes up."

Keith's head bobbed slightly, and his lanky form began to move toward where Shelby and Dylan stood in the doorway. He was a few feet from her when he said, "I'm really sorry about little Chad. It shouldn't have happened."

She had to strain to hear his soft voice. When she reached out to acknowledge his sentiment, Keith nearly flinched at the contact. It was his usual response. Whenever he was around Shelby, Keith acted like some sort of shy teenager.

A sudden burst of laughter floated up from the room below as Shelby crossed the thickly carpeted floor and took her place behind the cluttered desk. Rose was to her left, leaning against the credenza near the far wall. Dylan lingered at the edge of the desk, his hands resting on the surface.

"Tell me what happened."

Rose's head tilted to one side. The action allowed the harsh rays of sun spilling in from the window to glisten off the lacquered layer of hairspray. "Keith was the one who actually answered the phone. He turned it over to me when the guy said he was calling about Chad."

"And?"

Rose rubbed her upper arms and said, "His voice gave me the creeps. He said he was going to call back in thirty minutes, and you'd better be here. After he hung up, I called your place and told Williams."

Shelby glanced at the small oval clock on her desk. Any minute, she thought. But the minutes passed without the phone call. She began tapping her thumb against the desk, her fingers just inches from the receiver. *Come on!* she mentally pleaded. But still nothing.

When the intercom buzzed, Shelby nearly had to peel herself off the ceiling.

"What?" Rose barked into the small speaker.

"There's a new delivery guy here," Keith said. "He says he has to speak directly to one of the owners."

"Tell him I'm coming," Rose said, then moved toward the door, mumbling some rather unkind words under her breath.

As soon as Rose was gone, Dylan moved over to the other desk in the room.

"What are you doing?" Shelby demanded. He didn't respond. "That's Rose's desk."

"I figured that out for myself," he said as he slipped into the seat and opened the top drawer.

"You shouldn't be going through her things," she admonished.

"Under the circumstances," he began as he opened the second drawer, "I don't think she'll complain."

"You could have asked first," Shelby said. She looked again at the clock, then to the phone, then back to Dylan. Her patience was wearing thin. "Why doesn't he call?"

"He will," Dylan said. His attention remained on his task.

He hadn't even bothered to look up when he spoke. She could hear the rustle of papers, and she could just imagine how her partner would respond if she returned to find him elbow-deep in her private affairs.

"Why is this locked?"

She stood, her curiosity slowly edging out her impatience. "I don't know," she said as she walked around to where Dylan had rolled the chair back from the desk.

"Let's see what we have here."

She felt her eyes grow wide when he reached into his hip pocket and produced a small packet of long, thin metal picks. "You can't be thinking of picking the lock!"

He turned and looked up at her, his eyes sparkling with challenge. "Do you have a key?"

"No," she admitted quickly. "But you could show Rose the courtesy of asking her permission. She's just downstairs, for heaven's—"

The telephone came to life then, causing Shelby to jump.

"Are these connected?" Dylan asked as he pointed to the phone on Rose's desk.

"Yes."

"Grab the one on your desk. I'll listen in."

Shelby made a dash for the phone and grabbed it on the third ring. The cord tangled as she turned to watch Dylan as she spoke.

"Hello?"

"Nicely done, Shelby," the cryptic voice said. "You follow directions real good."

"Is Chad all right? Please let me talk to him."

"Patience, Shelby," he replied. "He's fine. So far."

She swallowed the lump of fear clogging her throat. Dylan nodded encouragingly when she made eye contact. She interpreted the motion as a sign of his support.

"Please don't hurt him."

"I'm not going to. Not unless you screw up."

"Just tell me what you want me to do," she said as she gripped the receiver in both hands. It was getting difficult to hear him over the sound of her pulse pounding in her ears.

"We're going to help each other, Shelby."

"Fine," she said quickly.

"I like saying your name, Shelby. Is it a family name?"

"My name isn't important!" she snapped. "Tell me what you want me to do to get my son back!"

She could hear him breathing, but it felt like several minutes before he said, "I want you to tell me about your name, Shelby. If you won't, I'll hang up."

"No! Please don't hang up," she breathed. "Shelby was my mother's maiden name."

"Fine Southern tradition, don't you think?"

"Yes."

"And what about Chad? Is Chad a family name, Shelby?"

"I named him after my father," she answered, without hesitation.

"He must have been proud."

"He's dead," she said flatly.

"I'm sorry about that, Shelby. Do you miss him?"

She bit her lip in an attempt to fend off the tears of frustration welling up in her eyes. "Yes, I miss him. We were very close."

"Like you and Chad?"

"Yes."

"Then I suppose we should do something about that, Shelby. How about it?"

"Anything."

"Then I'll be in touch."

"No! Wait!"

When she heard the distinctive click, Shelby closed her eyes and held the receiver to her chest.

"He's toying with you," Dylan told her as he quickly moved in front of her. "You did a good job, though. You were calm and cooperative. That'll almost guarantee he'll call back."

Her eyes opened, and he saw raw emotion in their blue depths. The pain ripped through his gut as he tried to think of something comforting to say. But there wasn't anything he could say. Nothing that could even come close to erasing the anguish he read on her face. Why the hell hadn't the CPD found Nichols yet? he wondered.

When she didn't move, he debated his next action. Swallowing once for courage, he reached out and placed his hands on her shoulders. He waited, not sure how she would interpret his actions. Hell, he wasn't even sure of his own motivations. But he decided it didn't really matter. Nothing mattered but his fierce need to protect her from Nichols and whoever his pathetic accomplice turned out to be.

With very little pressure, he eased her toward him, fully prepared for resistance. There was none. She fell against his chest, her hands still clasped around the telephone. He reached up and stroked her silky hair, wondering if she would fall to pieces. He'd been expecting tears since the beginning. At first he'd thought it was admirable that she'd been able to retain her composure. Now, however, he wasn't at all sure that stifling all her emotions was such a good idea.

"You can cry, you know."

She jerked back, out of his arms. Hard as it was, Dylan didn't do anything to counter her. He watched, almost helplessly, as she fell into the chair and leaned her head back against the cushion. Her body shuddered only slightly as she took in several large gulps of air.

"Did you recognize anything this time?"

"No," she answered in a small voice.

Nodding, Dylan moved back to the other desk and called Jay to fill him in.

"I don't like this," Jay said as soon as Dylan had recounted the gist of the conversation.

"Shelby wasn't real thrilled, either." He looked across at her as he spoke. She had picked up a framed photograph from her desk and was staring at the image of her child.

"This guy could be a kook," Jay continued. "All that stuff about her name—"

"It was weird," Dylan said, interrupting him. "I got the feeling the guy was out in left field, but we don't have much else to go on."

"There's Nichols," Jay countered.

"So why haven't we been able to find him?"

"His boat's gone from the marina. We've got men up and down the Ashley River looking for him."

"Find him fast," Dylan said in a near whisper. "I don't know how long she's going to be able to take this."

"Keep her there for a while," Jay instructed. "The guys from Southern Bell should be out there soon to set up the tap."

"Will do," Dylan said, and then hung up. She was still looking at the picture, and he had the feeling he should leave her alone with her thoughts.

He decided to busy himself by continuing his search through Rose's desk. The Porter woman wasn't the neatest female he'd run across. Her desk was filled with all sorts of interesting, though unimportant, things. He'd discovered an envelope filled with cereal-box tops, a pad of notepaper in the shape of a man's behind, and a whole collection of half-eaten rolls of antacids.

Nothing important, really—until he jimmied open the bottom drawer. His fingers ran across the faded label on the top of a bulging accordion file. He didn't recognize the name on it, but the word *Esquire* jumped out at him like a bright red flag.

Pulling the file from the drawer, he slid his thumbnail beneath the seam and ripped open the seal. He looked inside.

"What's that?"

"I don't know yet," he answered as he shook the papers out onto the desk top.

Shelby came over then, standing on the opposite side of the desk, with her arms crossed in front of her chest.

"Why don't you have Rose come up and go through that stuff with you?"

"You're one of the owners, so technically—" he lifted his eyes to hers "—unless you tell me I can't go through the desk, there's no legal expectation of privacy."

She shrugged, though indecision and uneasiness shone in her eyes. "It doesn't seem right...."

Her voice faded in his ears as he began to read the captions and skim the text of the documents. He felt his stomach knot with foreboding as he continued to read. Shelby began to speak, but he raised his hand in order to keep her quiet until he'd had an opportunity to finish.

When he finally looked up at her, he hoped his expression didn't reveal his true feelings. "We do need to get Rose up here."

"Why, Dylan?"

"Because she got three years from a Florida court for kidnapping."

Chapter Five

"Where's Rose?" Shelby demanded as she grabbed a handful of Keith's shirtsleeve.

The lanky young man's eyes flew open, but he remained mute.

"I asked you where—"

"She ran out of here about fifteen minutes ago."

Shelby turned away from the chef and peered around Dylan's rather imposing shoulders.

Tory Conway stood with her foot holding the shiny metal door at an angle. An empty tray was balanced against her nearly nonexistent hip.

"Where did she go?"

Tory entered the kitchen and shoved an order ticket into the chrome carousel before automatically giving the thing a spin. "I don't have a clue," she said on a breath. "She just ran past me as I was coming in for my shift."

"Who are you?" Dylan asked in a deep voice.

Shelby watched as Tory's dark blue eyes roamed over Dylan's handsome face. The younger woman's head angled to one side, and her expression seemed to cloud defensively.

She told him her name and added, "I work here. Unless that's a problem."

Dylan seemed taken aback by the challenge in the tiny woman's tone. Shelby could almost feel him stiffen in response to the defiant tilt of Tory's chin.

He turned and looked to her for verification. Shelby nodded and said, "Tory works evenings as a waitress."

"Tory is working harder this evening, because it doesn't seem as if anyone else around here does squat," Tory grumbled.

Keith piped up. "Because of what happened to Chad."

Tory's features softened instantly, and she immediately made eye contact with Shelby. "Chad got hurt?" she asked, moving a few steps closer.

"Someone took him," Shelby managed. Saying it out loud was amazingly painful. It had a certain finality to it that sent a shiver of renewed fear the full length of her spine.

"God! Shelby!" Tory ran a hand through her stylishly short blond hair. "I had no idea."

"I tried to tell you," Keith whined, in a tone reminiscent of sibling one-upmanship.

Tory cast him a withering look before she asked, "How? When?"

"Last night," Dylan answered. "Sometime after nine."

Tory leaned against the countertop and abandoned her tray with a loud clanging. "This is terrible."

"Yes," Dylan agreed, "it is."

"What can I do?" Tory asked.

"You can start by telling me where you were last night between eight and midnight," Dylan said.

His question seemed to take Tory by surprise. She blinked twice before beginning to speak. "I was right here until two this morning."

"I can vouch for that," Keith chimed in.

Shelby could have sworn something passed between her two employees, but whatever it was, or wasn't, it hadn't lasted long enough for her to give it a definition.

One of the swinging doors flew open and banged against the wall.

Erica, one of the other waitresses, leaned forward and yelled, "Hey, Tory! The deuce by the door wants you, now!"

"Shelby, I—"

"Go on," Shelby said, interrupting her.

Tory gave her a weak smile, and she was vaguely aware of the fact that the woman squeezed her arm before racing out into the dining area.

Dylan turned to face the cook. Keith was on the opposite side of the long stainless-steel counter that spanned nearly the entire length of the kitchen. He saw a thin sheen of moisture on the man's upper lip. He noted the slight tremor in the guy's bony hand.

"You need anything, Shelby?" Keith asked in a small voice.

Dylan saw her shake her head in his peripheral vision.

"When did you say Rose left?"

Keith looked up at him then. His pale eyes were surprisingly angry. "About twenty minutes ago, now. Just before the phone rang."

"And she didn't say where she was going?" Dylan pressed.

Keith shook his head. "Nope. She just read the note and bolted."

"*What* note?"

Both Keith and Shelby started at the harsh edge in his voice, which he couldn't manage to keep in check.

"From the delivery guy."

"She ran out of here because of something the delivery-eryman gave her?"

Keith shifted his weight from foot to foot and bowed his head. "I think he was one of them."

"Well?" Dylan slapped his hand on the counter in front of him. The bustle of activity in the kitchen came to a sudden halt. "Was the note from a delivery person or not?"

Keith slowly raised his head and looked pleadingly at Shelby before giving Dylan his reluctant attention. "He came in with them, so I thought he was with them."

"And then what?" Dylan prompted.

"He told me he needed to speak with Mrs. Porter. Said she was the only one he could speak to."

"What did he look like?"

Keith's forehead drew together beneath his chef's hat as he thought about his answer. "He was just a kid. Maybe fifteen or sixteen."

"Height? Weight?" Dylan asked, pulling a small note-book from the back pocket of his jeans.

"About your height."

Dylan made a note. Six feet three inches.

"Thin, like me."

He added an estimated weight of 180 to his note. "Anything special about this kid?"

"No."

Dylan flipped the cover closed with a flick of his wrist, and let out a breath of frustration. He turned to find Shelby leaning against the wall. The black hair framing her face reflected the afternoon sunlight, much as it had that afternoon so long ago. . . .

"ARE WE ALLOWED to take picnics on government time?"

Shifting the basket to his other hand, Dylan reached out and caught her around the waist. He loved the feel of the soft fabric of her blouse. His mind instantly began to wonder about what was beneath the material. It was a path his thoughts had taken over and over during the course of their time together. He was fascinated by everything about her—her delicate features, the way her eyes grew large when she laughed, the shy way she smiled when she caught him looking at her.

"Just think of this as your tax dollars at work," he teased, bending low enough to catch the scent of her perfume on the warm breeze.

"Does this mean I'm responsible for the unchecked growth of the deficit?"

She looked up at him with those stunning blue eyes, and he nearly tripped over his own foot. He felt like some sort of overgrown teenager caught in the throes of first love. He had all the signs—sweaty palms, the inability to keep that simpleton's grin off his face. And then there was the matter of his jeans, which grew increasingly more uncomfortable the longer he was in the company of Shelby.

"Is this okay?"

She stopped suddenly as she asked the question. Dylan couldn't stop quickly enough, and found himself plastered against her. It wasn't exactly an unpleasant predicament, but he cleared his throat and regained his balance.

"Excellent choice," he told her as he placed the basket on the ground, and made a production out of scanning the nicely secluded spot she'd chosen for their lunch.

When she leaned over to smooth out the blanket, Dylan was treated to a view of her backside. He found it far more interesting than the topography of the park. Her jeans clung lovingly to her shapely hips and hugged her slightly rounded derriere. Her blouse had worked its way *free from the waistband, revealing just a hint of creamy white skin.*

"*Start grabbing things,*" she said.

"WE HAVE TO FIND ROSE," Dylan said as he slid onto one of the high stools at the bar.

"I can't believe Rose would do anything like this to me."

The bartender placed a cup of coffee in front of her, then somberly took Dylan's order. The din of voices gave Shelby an odd sense of comfort. She supposed it had something to do with her emotional connection to the bar. The Rose Tattoo had given Shelby a sense of belonging when she desperately needed security.

Elvis Presley's voice crooned softly from the jukebox, which was audible above the faint crackling of the logs burning in the fireplace.

"She has a lot of explaining to do."

"You saw her, Dylan," she said as she angled herself on the stool, crossing one leg over the other. "Rose has a few rough edges, but she isn't capable of doing anything like kidnapping my son."

"You have an incredible knack for only seeing the best in people."

"And you always seem to look for the worst," she returned.

His jaw tensed, but he still didn't take his eyes off her. The pleasant scent of his cologne reached out to soothe her frazzled nerves. *Why am I jumping down his throat?* she wondered as she gripped the warm ceramic mug full of coffee with both hands.

"I called Jay and told him about the papers I found."

She felt her mouth drop open. "Why did you do that before we've had an opportunity to talk to her?"

"Because I thought—"

The chirping sound of the phone cut him off in mid-sentence.

Josh reached beneath the bar and brought the extension to her reach. Shelby grabbed it on the second ring. "Rose Tattoo."

"Hi, Shelby."

The icy fingers of fear gripped her throat, and she waved her hand in front of Dylan to get his attention. "It's him!" she mouthed.

Dylan swiveled on his seat. Shelby braced herself, placing her free hand on the bar.

"Is Chad all right?" she managed, in a deceptively calm voice.

"Of course he's all right, Shelby," the male voice replied. "I told you nothing would happen so long as you followed my instructions."

Dylan leaned close enough that he, too, could listen to the tormenting voice.

"You haven't given me any instructions."

"I suppose you're right," he said after a short pause. "But I'm ready now."

"Anything!" she gushed. "I'll do anything to get my son back!"

"You really love that kid, don't you?"

"Of course I do."

"How much?"

She blinked and said, "What do you mean? He's my child! I love him more than my own life!"

"No, no, Shelby," he said with a humorless laugh. "I don't mean philosophically. I'm talking dollars here."

"Dollars?" she repeated.

Dylan gripped her wrist and gave a squeeze. She met his gray eyes and watched as he signaled her to agree to whatever the demand might be.

"N-name your price."

She could almost hear a satisfied smirk as he said, "Good, Shelby. I always thought you were an exceptional businesswoman."

"What made you think that?"

"You always treated folks decently."

"At the Tattoo?"

His snort of laughter frightened her. Had she pushed him too far? Asked too many questions?

"I've really enjoyed our time together."

"What about my son?" she demanded. "Has he been well cared for?"

"I told you the kid was fine," he shot back impatiently. "And he'll be home before bedtime, if you do exactly as I say."

"I will."

"Do you know the Tennison Packing Plant on River Road?"

"Yes."

"Bring fifty thousand dollars cash there at eight o'clock tonight."

"Fifty thousand dollars?" she repeated.

Shelby looked up to see Dylan nodding furiously.

"Is that a problem?"

"No," she assured him. "No problem."

"And, Shelby?"

"Yes."

"No cops, or you'll never see your little boy again."

She stared at the silent phone for a few seconds before replacing it on the cradle. Dylan reached out and placed his hand on her thigh. She felt the heat of his touch as she fought to keep from crumbling then and there. She actually considered blurting out her secret. She wanted someone to share her pain and her fear.

"Do you think he was telling the truth?"

As usual, he only shrugged his broad shoulders. "We'll know tonight at eight." He took his hand away and used it to lift his glass of cola to his lips. "We've got just about enough time to make the arrangements for the money—"

"How am I supposed to get my hands on fifty thousand dollars in a little over four hours?"

The muscles in his face relaxed then.

"We'll take care of that."

"But what about what he said?" she all but screamed. Then, realizing she was attracting the attention of some of the patrons, she lowered her voice. "If he sees any police, he'll hurt Chad!"

"He won't see us, Shelby."

"How can you be so sure?"

He looked at her then. Turned those intense eyes on her without warning. "You'll just have to trust me."

His words were still ringing in her ears when Jay Williams entered the dining room. He and a handful of other officers weaved through the early dinner crowd and joined them at the bar. Josh acknowledged them by placing napkins in front of each man.

"Where's Mrs. Porter?" Jay asked them, his elbows resting on the bar.

"She hasn't come back yet," Dylan answered.

Jay's expression soured at the news, and he slapped one hand against his leg in frustration.

"I made arrangements for a couple of the city boys to wait at your house in case she shows up there."

"Do you have the papers you mentioned on the phone?"

Dylan shook his head, causing some of his ebony hair to spill across his brow. Shelby fought the urge to reach up and brush it back into place.

"I left them upstairs. I didn't think we'd need them."

Jay's expression went past sour, all the way toward hostile. "I would like an opportunity to—"

"I got another call, just a minute ago," Shelby said, interrupting. She didn't like listening to Jay berate Dylan.

"Another call?"

She nodded at him and said, "He called to let me know he wants me to meet him at Tennison's tonight."

"With fifty grand," Dylan added.

"And I have to go alone."

Jay slowly slumped against the back of one stool. Both hands came up to rake through his neat pile of wavy brown hair. His eyes clouded over, as if he were totally perplexed. Shelby wondered what he knew that he wasn't telling.

"Oh, thank God!" Rose bellowed.

Rose burst into the room, clutching something to her chest and struggling for gulps of air.

Dylan was the first to reach her. Without preamble, he pulled the brown paper sack from her hand and roughly tugged her toward the group.

"What do you think you're doing?" Rose barked as she steadied herself.

Shelby couldn't stand to see her friend being badly treated, so she tried to move past Dylan. He wasn't having any of it.

"Where did you disappear to?" he demanded.

Rose blinked once, and then the expression in her eyes grew wary. "I was doing you a favor."

"How so?"

"That!" she yelped as she waved her hand in the direction of the paper bag.

Williams grabbed the bag from Dylan and reached inside. She watched him slowly pull a videotape from inside.

"It looks like another one," he said after a brief examination.

He was in the process of handing it to Dylan when Shelby stepped up and snatched it away. "You can analyze it to death— *after* I've watched it."

With the lot of them on her heels, Shelby led the procession to her office. The tape was placed in the machine connected to the small television set behind her desk, and in a few seconds the image began to appear.

As Chad's smiling face filled the small screen, Shelby felt Dylan's hand close over her shoulder. Rose lowered herself onto the edge of the desk, next to her. They all stared silently at the television.

"That's Waterfront Park!" Shelby exclaimed when she recognized the area where the stroller her son sat in was parked.

"That's less than three blocks from here," Rose added.

Suddenly a hand came into the shot. It was the same woman's hand as in the first videotape. At least the ring looked the same. The hand placed a newspaper in front of the baby. The camera zoomed in for a close-up of the date.

"Today's *Centennial*," Dylan said.

The baby managed to get hold of a corner of the paper. His squeal of delight at his accomplishment was both reassuring and heart-wrenching for Shelby.

The camera angle widened, giving her a full view of the baby. He was dressed in what she could only have described as an adorable outfit—one she knew wasn't his. His broad smile was contagious and she felt the corners of her mouth curve upward.

"Da, da, da, da."

The tape ended on the sobering sound of Chad's babbling.

"Did you hear that?" Dylan asked excitedly.

Lifting her chin, Shelby looked up at him, confused.

"Was he saying 'daddy'?"

She averted her eyes and said, "Of course not."

"But you heard him say—"

"He's a baby, Dylan. Babies speak gibberish like that all the time."

"A lot like you guys," Rose said in a stage whisper.

Jay cut off the set, and he and Dylan stood in front of them. Dylan crossed his arms in front of his chest, and glared down at Rose.

Shelby turned to see that Rose was glaring right back.

"It's come to our attention that you were involved in a kidnapping in Florida," Jay began.

Rose flinched, and her shoulders slumped forward slightly. "I guess I should have told one of you about that."

"It isn't true, is it, Rose?" Shelby gasped, placing her hand to her open mouth.

"It isn't what they've no doubt led you to believe," she answered quickly. "It's not like I'm some sort of criminal or anything."

"A Florida court didn't see it that way," Jay countered.

"I got three years probation," Rose told him. "It wasn't any big deal."

"Kidnapping is usually considered a big deal," Dylan suggested rather snidely. "Parents like to know where their children are."

Rose got to her feet and stood toe-to-toe with Dylan. Placing her hands on her hips, she tilted her head back and said, "But they were my children."

Chapter Six

"Your children?" Shelby queried through her confusion.

Rose's head bobbed furiously up and down. Shelby was only vaguely aware of the others in the room as she silently struggled to overcome the shock of hearing such an incredible revelation.

"It wasn't like they're making it out," she insisted.

When Shelby looked into her friend's eyes, she discovered they were wide, almost pleading in their intensity. "But you took—"

"I didn't do anything wrong!" she insisted. "Listen," Rose said, tugging on the sleeve of Shelby's blouse. "I had my kids young. Too young." Her head dipped fractionally, and her expression clouded, as if she were actually traveling back into the memories.

"Joe Don and me, we just sort of drifted apart."

"But the children?" Shelby prompted.

"Two boys," Rose said softly. The small smile that curved her bright fuchsia lips was bittersweet and tight.

"You're divorced?" Dylan asked.

For the first time in several minutes, Shelby lifted her head and looked in his direction. He leaned against the bar, his massive arms crossed in front of his equally impressive chest. Fatigue registered around the corners of his gray-blue eyes. More of his dark hair had fallen forward on his forehead. Rich rays of golden sunlight spilled in from the window, creating shadows that softened the sharp angles of his features.

"Of course I'm divorced," Rose said on a sigh. "Joe Don Porter became Joseph Porter. And Joseph Porter became an architect who didn't need or want me as a wife."

Shelby patted her friend's hand. "It happens," she said, then instantly felt foolish for having said something so trite.

"This is all very interesting, Mrs. Porter," Jay said. "But your marital woes don't explain the circumstances of—"

"I'm getting to it!" Rose snapped.

Shelby could feel the other woman's slight body tense as she shifted her weight from foot to foot. The sound of the heels of her shoes scuffing the carpet preceded her words.

"Joe Don and me used to be a lot alike."

With thick, sluggish movements, Rose began to pace. For the first time, Shelby noted that Rose's normally confident shoulders had slumped forward. That almost defiant wiggle was gone from her walk.

"He went to night school while I waited tables," Rose continued as she fingered a small pile of pale pink napkins embossed with the rose logo of the restaurant. "J.D. and Wesley were just out of diapers when Joe Don decided he needed a change."

Rose turned then, her eyes narrowed and full of long-held fury. "Of course, part of the change included a young, pretty coed he'd met."

"That's terrible," Shelby managed.

Rose snorted. "Not really. After the initial shock wore off, I was just as glad to be rid of him."

"Could you get to the part about the children?" Jay asked, without bothering to disguise his impatience.

"The boys and me were fine. I was working, making decent tips." Rose turned her back and began rubbing her hands along the sides of her arms. "The manager let me keep the boys in a playpen on the top floor during my shift."

"You kept two toddlers at a bar?" Dylan asked.

His question earned him a sharp look from Shelby. She wondered if the man had any earthly idea what it was like to be a working mother.

"I kept food in their mouths and clothes on their backs," Rose answered. "We didn't hear a peep from Joe Don until nearly two years later. He'd married his coed. They had a successful architectural firm in south Florida. And they wanted my kids."

Shelby swallowed and closed her eyes for a brief second. She knew instantly how Rose must have felt all those years ago.

"He and the coed took me to court."

"You lost custody of the boys?"

Rose's mirthless laugh sent a chill the full length of Shelby's spine.

"Hell, no, I didn't lose custody. At least not here in South Carolina."

"You were charged in Florida," Dylan put in gently.

"The judge here said I had to let them have the boys for summer visits. I did. The kids were with them for almost three months. Joe Don and the coed used their influence down in Florida to pull some fancy legal stuff. The next thing I knew, some weasely process server shows up on my doorstep with papers that say I have to appear in court for a custody hearing."

"What happened in Florida?" Jay asked.

"I wouldn't know," Rose answered. Her shoulders fell forward another fraction. "I ran right down there and got my boys."

Shelby felt the muscles in her face relax.

"I didn't even get as far as the Georgia border before the cops pulled me over and arrested me."

"How awful," Shelby moaned.

"It took months for all the court stuff. By then, the boys had been with Joe Don and the coed for so long that this psychology woman told the courts that it would be harmful for them to be returned to me."

"Did you fight him?" The question came from Dylan.

Rose nodded and said, "At first. Then I went and saw them at their father's place." She grew silent for a few minutes, her fingers nervously twisting the chain of plastic beads hanging from her neck. "They each had their own room. They had nice clothes, a house with a yard and a pool."

"So you decided to leave them with your ex-husband," Jay concluded.

"Joe Don and the coed were...persuasive," she admitted. "They wouldn't take my word that I'd leave the boys with them. That's why they didn't back off the kidnapping thing. But I would have done what was right for the boys even without their threats."

The last statement was delivered in a barely audible whisper. Sucking in a deep breath, Rose went through a remarkable transformation, right before Shelby's eyes.

Her posture straightened, and that air of belligerent confidence returned, as Rose spun and faced her. The chain of beads dangled from the tip of one long red fingernail.

"So you see," she said, only to Shelby, "there's no way I could be involved with little Chad's disappearance."

"I know that," Shelby said as she moved to hug her friend. "I never believed you were involved, Rose."

"DAMN IT!" Dylan yelled as he jumped away from the stream of hot water spewing from the shower head. His skin burned where he had stupidly allowed the water to scald him. He let out a few additional expletives as he adjusted the knob.

"Lack of sleep," he told the mixed-breed that came bounding around the corner.

The dog's nails slid and scraped the tile just before he caromed into the side of the tub. Dylan snickered at the dog's stupidity. "No wonder I've kept you all these years, Foolish," he said as he patted the stubby hair on the top of the animal's head. "We have something in common." He slipped into the shower and pulled the vinyl curtain closed. "Neither one of us can do two things at once. I can't think and turn on the shower, and you can't walk and . . . do anything."

Foolish barked once before insinuating his elongated snout on the edge of the tub. Dylan looked down and tried to keep a straight face, the way his neighbor, Miss Dog Expert, had instructed.

"Get down. You're getting water on the floor."

The dog looked up with his eyes, but no other part of him moved.

He searched his memory to recall what Miss Dog Expert had told him to do when Foolish ignored his command. He couldn't remember a damned word, so he improvised.

"I said, get down." He punctuated the remark by spritzing the dog with just a few drops of water.

It worked—sort of. Foolish shook his head and left the bathroom, but not before he captured the towel in his teeth and dragged it off to God knew where.

"Your life has gone to hell," he muttered as he allowed the water to massage the stiff muscles between his shoulder blades. He had pretty much resigned himself to the fact that Shelby was a part of his past. Until he had seen her again.

His hands reached up to lather the shampoo. "She has a baby," he muttered. "*And* she has a life."

Dylan continued to mentally berate himself as he showered. That sick, selfish part of his mind had always hoped that she was as miserable without him as he'd been since the night she'd told him it was over. He wanted to believe that Shelby had regretted ending their short-lived relationship and was secretly longing for him.

"It turns out that's about as likely as you learning to behave," he told the dog as he walked, naked and dripping, toward his dresser. "I don't suppose you'd like to cough up the towel?"

Foolish barked loudly, and his tail thumped against the floor.

"Thank you," Dylan said with a sneer. "The next time I run, you stay home."

The dog barked again.

"I'm threatening you," he told the dog as he began pulling clothing from the dresser and the closet. "I'm taking away your privileges. You're grounded."

The dog's tail beat more enthusiastically.

"You're supposed to look humble, and slink off into a corner and wait for me to forgive you."

Foolish sneezed.

"Thanks," Dylan said, patting the animal. "Obviously I have as much luck with animals as I do with women."

Foolish followed him into the kitchen and made a general nuisance of himself as Dylan tried to put together something that resembled a sandwich. He had to be quick, though. The dog believed in self-service, so nothing was safe. Not the cheese, not the bread, not even the condiments.

Dylan sat at the small round table that fit awkwardly into one corner. The dog was just a few inches away, poised and ready.

Reaching into a bowl in the center of the table, Dylan plucked up a few grapes. He ate one, then tossed the other in the air. Foolish snagged it as it arced.

"She looked incredible, even under the circumstances," he said as he alternated between eating and tossing grapes to the dog. "None of this makes any sense, pal."

He carried his half-eaten sandwich with him when he went to the refrigerator for a bottle of water.

"That's why it has to be Ned. He must have found out about the baby. It's the only possible explanation."

Foolish whined, apparently in protest against the interruption in his feeding. "But the medallion is what gets me," he continued, thinking aloud. He could feel deep lines of concentration gather between his brows. "Why would a medallion, that looks like the one I lost, suddenly turn up at the scene of a kidnapping? If it had to turn up, why there? Why at Shelby's?"

He pushed the plate away from him and leaned back in the seat. The thin wooden slats creaked in protest against his size. The clock above the stove told him he had less than an hour to pick up the cash and meet Shelby back at her place for the drop.

"If Ned took the baby, then Ned planted the medallion," he reasoned. Shaking his head, he said, "But Ned didn't have access to my medallion. Which means it can't be mine. If it wasn't mine, then Ned fits.''

But nothing else does, he thought. *Not by a long shot.* As he pulled a pair of black jeans, Dylan was still trying to make some sense out of what he knew. Unfortunately, the image of Shelby kept interfering with his ability to think clearly and precisely. Even at the worst possible time in her life, she was the most beautiful woman he'd ever seen. She had the ability to tie his gut into a knot just by making eye contact. He'd never reacted to a woman the way he reacted to her, and he didn't like it.

His long-suppressed feelings for her were clouding his ability to use his brain effectively. He should be thinking about motives and opportunity, but he was still stuck on the issue of the baby. He knew it was wrong, but he felt something far too much like betrayal when he allowed himself to acknowledge that Shelby and Nichols had created a child together.

"You're being stupid," he cautioned himself as he pulled a black sweater over his shirt. "It wasn't like you were engaged to her," he told his frowning reflection.

"Things just got out of hand," he said, mimicking Shelby's voice as he repeated the words she'd said to him.

After brushing his still-damp hair, Dylan grabbed his keys and took the dog out for a quick walk. Then he headed out.

With the money safely tucked inside a nylon bag on the seat next to him, Dylan weaved his way through the city traffic, toward Shelby's place. His mind kept volleying between thoughts of her and his analysis of the crime. Part of him wanted it to end, and end quickly. They'd pay the ransom, pick up the kid and arrest Nichols, then they could part company for good.

Another part of him hated the thought of walking out of her life for a second time. Even more, he hated the fact that in both instances Ned Nichols had been the catalyst. His grip tightened on the wheel as he fantasized about what he'd like to do to the slime when they finally tracked him down.

Jay was waiting for him when he turned onto the street. He would have preferred Shelby.

"We've located Nichols," Jay announced as soon as Dylan emerged from the car.

Chapter Seven

Late afternoon had brought with it a series of dark, moisture-ladened clouds that Shelby watched from the window as a sense of foreboding settled over the room. Her eyes were drawn to Dylan, who stood in the driveway, engrossed in animated conversation with Jay.

There was a time when she had dreamed of him walking back into her life. Her fantasy had never included any of this. "Why is this happening?" she whispered as her eyes closed to fight off the threat of tears.

There wasn't any answer, just as there was no explanation for so many things. Why Chad? Why now? And why had a medallion that looked like Dylan's turned up in the bushes?

Now that she was adjusting to the situation, her mind was beginning to function, despite the numbness. She had some private misgivings about Ned. But they had nothing to do with his supposed connection to arms deals. "And they certainly don't have anything to do with Chad."

Moving away from the window, Shelby picked up her brush and began the process of gathering her hair into a barrette at the back of her neck. Her hair was still damp from her hurried shower, and she wasn't in any frame of mind to do much with it.

Her thoughts kept analyzing what little she knew. Desperation slowly gave way to determination as she pulled on a pair of jeans. It couldn't be Ned. No way.

Dylan and the rest of them were convinced it was Ned acting on some surge of parental emotion. Shelby felt herself frown as she acknowledged the many flaws in that conclusion. First, Ned had no reason to think he was Chad's father. Second, in spite of Dylan's delusions in that area, Ned had never treated her with anything other than professional interest. Until she'd opened the purchase orders by mistake. Maybe she should have told Dylan everything. Now that wasn't even a possibility.

A succession of rapid knocks interrupted her thoughts. She was pushing the bottom edge of her sweater into the waistband of her jeans as she went to the door.

The sight of Dylan dressed head to toe in black was enough to still the breath in her throat. He loomed in the shadowy hallway, his broad shoulders diffusing the light from the first floor.

"There's been a new development."

Shelby reached out and grasped his forearm, her eyes meeting and holding his.

"Nichols has been located."

She didn't react. He wasn't sure what he had expected, but it hadn't been this bland poker face. *God,* he thought as he battled to keep a sneer off his face. Her feelings for Nichols were obviously strong enough that she was willing to accept the kidnapping of her son as just another of the guy's minor character flaws.

"Don't you want to know where he is?"

He saw her expression stiffen in response to the anger he seemed incapable of keeping out of his tone. Her eyes widened with astonishment, almost making him regret the derision in his voice.

"Where is he?" she asked after a long silence.

"Istanbul."

"Turkey?"

It wasn't really a question, so he didn't bother with an answer.

Actually, he was more distracted by watching her move than he was by the lack of emotion in her voice. He hated himself for noticing the flattering fit of her clothing, but that didn't stop him from looking. When she turned her back to him, Dylan allowed his gaze to slide slowly over every inch of her. He tried to tell himself that he was just doing his job. Just making sure she'd chosen an appropriate outfit to meet the caller.

It was crap, and he knew it. There was no such thing as a dress code for paying off a kidnapper. He lowered his eyes and swallowed some of his guilt.

"Ned goes to Turkey several times a year."

He looked up to find her taking things out of her handbag, and placing them in a black leather fanny pack on the bed.

"Does he usually go by way of Savannah?"

She turned and faced him then, her perfectly shaped brows drawn together in a question. "S-Savannah?" she stammered.

Dylan felt himself relax. He was most comfortable when he had control of the situation. It was an elusive concept whenever Shelby was around, so he savored the moment. "Apparently he took his boat down to the Atlantic, sailed to Savannah. Took a flight to Heathrow. Then on to Istanbul."

This new information had taken her by surprise. He could tell by her body language.

"What about the package he was supposed to have had when he was seen leaving his house?"

Dylan cleared his throat and shifted his glance to a collection of brightly colored glass bottles on top of her dressing table.

"He didn't have it when he went through customs in London."

"So he can't possibly have Chad," she said with conviction.

"He didn't when he went through customs," Dylan admitted. "But that doesn't—"

"And if he's been on boats and planes and heaven only knows what else since before midnight yesterday, then he can't be the one sending the tapes and making the calls."

"Shelby," he said as he moved next to her. Cautiously he placed his hands firmly on her shoulders and forced her to make direct eye contact. "We've assumed all along that there's more than one individual involved. Everything about this case indicates that there is more than one individual pulling the strings."

"How do *we* know that? And why are you so sure one of them is Ned?"

His hands gave a gentle squeeze and he said, "Well, Ned is your only enemy—plus, there's too many jobs for just one perp."

"Jobs?"

Dylan withdrew his hands and used the fingers of his left hand to count off each point. "Access was gained through the nursery window. We found impressions of a ladder in the soil beneath the window."

"How does that tell you there were two kidnappers?"

"The indentations were of approximately equal depths."

"Meaning?"

"Meaning that, in all likelihood, someone was holding the ladder on the ground."

He watched the faint flicker of pain flash in her blue eyes, and began to question the advisability of getting into all this with her.

"What else?"

"It isn't really important, Shelby."

"It is to me," she told him quietly, her eyes pleading for his cooperation.

"The videotapes require at least two people—the camera operator and the mysterious woman with the ring."

"Couldn't they be taken using a tripod?" Shelby asked.

Dylan shook his head and said, "The lab guys say no. They say the movement of the lens position is inconsistent with the use of a stable base."

She smiled at him. He found it contagious.

"They like it when you quote them exactly," he admitted with a sheepish grin.

"You're very good at it. You sounded just like some boring report."

"Boring, huh?" he teased, feigning great indignation.

Her smile grew wider, and he noted just the palest tinge of color appear on the flawlessly opaque skin near her high cheekbones. Her lashes fluttered just before she lowered her eyes.

"I didn't mean it like that."

"I know it," Dylan responded.

"What else?" she asked as she returned her attention to packing items into the largest of the compartments of the fanny pack.

"There's the problem of the tapes and the calls."

"Problem?"

"It's not exactly the standard in cases like this."

"There's a standard?" she asked.

He felt a tug in his chest at the almost pitiful sentiment behind the statement. "It's like overkill, Shelby. Neither I or Jay have ever heard of a case where so much contact was initiated by the perp. You can expect calls. You can expect tapes. But never both.''

Her expression clouded over with uneasiness. "And you think this is a bad sign?"

"No," he said on a rush of air. "I'm not saying anything of the kind." He placed his hand on her arm, silently wishing there was some way he could comfort away the shimmer of tears he saw pooling in her eyes.

"Personally, I think it's a good sign that these people are so hell-bent on proving to you that Chad is doing okay."

She held on to his words as if they were some sort of lifeline. It was far superior to allowing her own thoughts to wander.

"But why have you and Jay decided that no matter what the evidence, Ned has to be one of the individuals involved?"

She could see his expression darken in her peripheral vision. At least he's consistent, she thought as she buckled the leather pouch around her waist.

"Motive, Shelby. That, and the fact that we haven't been able to come up with a single lead in any other direction. It would appear that you've managed to live your life without making any enemies."

Except you, she thought dismally. "I've been telling you that from the beginning."

"What about when you and Ned were working together?"

"What do you mean?" she said as she brushed past him.

"Did you ever have it out with a customer? Pad the markup?"

She stopped just short of the door, her back stiff. "Of course not, Dylan. We sold imported items, and the occasional antiquity. They were all big-ticket items, and our customers were educated and informed. We sold many items to museums and universities.''

"Thanks for the résumé," he muttered.

Shelby ignored the sarcasm in his tone. She'd accomplished her mission. Dylan's anger was preventing him pressing the issue any further.

"We have everything in place," Jay announced as soon as they reached the landing. "I've verified that everyone's in position, and we've decided to kill the radios, just in case our man is listening in."

"Are you sure he won't know you're there?" Shelby asked for the hundredth time. "I couldn't live with myself if anything happened to my baby because I didn't follow his instructions to a T."

"Don't worry," Jay said, placing a fatherly arm across her shoulders. "We've done this more times than I'd like to remember. There's no way this fruit will know we're within ten miles of the packing plant. He'll show for the goods. We'll nab him, and he can spend the rest of his useless life in some stinking prison cell."

Shelby looked up, and nearly flinched at the hostility she read in the man's eyes. "Didn't you forget something?" she asked cautiously.

"What?" Jay snapped.

"Getting him to tell us where he's hiding Chad?"

Jay's dark eyes narrowed, and the small smile of reassurance he offered failed to reach his eyes. "Of course we'll find the baby, Shelby."

"Are you sure he won't be able to see *him* in the car?"

Dylan made some sort of unflattering noise. She guessed he didn't like being referred to as "him."

"He'll be in the back seat. Tanner knows the drill. He won't compromise the situation."

I'm still worried about him, she thought. Just being around Dylan was unnerving. Shelby wasn't at all sure she could function with him literally at her feet.

"The money is in the gym bag," Jay said. "All you have to do is park and wait."

Nodding, Shelby pulled out her car keys and placed her slightly trembling hand on the cool doorknob.

"Relax, Shelby."

She turned to take one final look at Jay. His face was impassive, only his dark eyes hinting at something more. Her throat constricted. There was something about Jay's demeanor that wasn't right.

The smile he offered was weak, and did nothing to alleviate her budding misgivings.

"We'll be right there with you," Jay assured her. "No matter what."

"Will you explain Jay to me?" she asked after backing her car out of the drive.

"Jay's beyond explanation" came Dylan's muffled reply.

"Is it me, or did he seem less than enthusiastic about all this?"

Dylan didn't respond immediately, which only added to her growing insecurities.

"That's just his way. He's reserved."

His voice had an oddly immediate soothing effect on her nerves as she steered out of the city, toward the appointed drop site. A thick layer of clouds obscured the sunset, bringing on a premature darkness.

Bohicket Road, a winding strip of macadam in dire need of repairs, was all but deserted. Each pothole was tallied by Dylan's grunt of discomfort. She could only imagine how cramped he must be, his large body folded into the small space between the front seat and the back seat.

"Are you sure you wouldn't be more comfortable up here?" she asked. "At least until we're closer to Tennisons?"

"Too dangerous."

"How so?"

"This guy may be watching. It's better to play it safe."

Shelby immediately checked the rearview mirror. Not a car in sight. She told Dylan.

"He could be watching from the roadside. Or come from the opposite direction. I don't think you want to risk annoying this guy."

"Definitely not," she agreed. "I just want my son back."

Dylan fell silent. Her only indication that he was in the car was the gentle rustling of the blanket whenever he shifted his position.

"Why'd you do it?" he asked, in a deep, soft voice.

"Do what?"

"Decide to have the kid."

Her hands tightened on the wheel, her knuckles turning white. "It wasn't a decision."

"An accident?"

There was an edge to the question that only added to her apprehensions. "I prefer to think of Chad as a surprise. *Accident* carries the connotation that he wasn't wanted. He was."

"So why not do it the traditional way?"

"It didn't happen that way," she returned shortly. "I'd appreciate it if you'd drop it."

"Sorry."

But she could tell he wasn't. Was he beginning to put it together?

"I hope not."

"You hope not what?" he asked.

Realizing she had spoken her fears aloud, Shelby cleared her throat anxiously and said, "I hope I haven't made a mistake by involving all of you in this. I meant what I said, Dylan. I won't be able to live with myself if anything happens to Chad."

"I won't let anything happen to him. I promise."

God! she thought as she flipped the turn signal and prepared to turn into the lot. He sounded so sincere, so concerned. *How will he feel if he learns the truth?*

She banished such thoughts as she eased the car across the uneven gravel lot. The air was thick with the scent of damp cardboard and rotting produce. It was fully dark now, her headlights the only source of illumination.

A chill danced along her spine. "We're here."

"See anything?" he asked in a whisper.

"Everything's dark. I can barely make out the buildings."

"Turn your lights out," he instructed. "Let your eyes adjust to the dark."

Following his directives, Shelby blinked against the darkness until the formless shadows began to take shape. A loading dock, three Dumpsters, and several towers of packing crates lining the parking area.

Her eyes darted in all directions, trying to find some evidence that her tormentor was there.

"Roll down the window, see if you can hear anything."

"Like what?" she whispered.

"A baby crying."

Depressing the button, she lowered the window, then cut the engine. She listened intently for some sound to emerge over the chorus of insects. She held her breath. Nothing.

"I don't hear anything," she whispered.

Dylan's hand snaked between the door and the seat to rest on the side of her hip. The contact was equal measures comforting and disturbing. She swallowed some of her dread.

"What should I do?"

"Wait."

She could hardly hear him above the sounds of the crickets.

There was a rustling sound to the left of the car. Shelby whipped her head around and held her breath.

Her eyes fixed on something—movement in the thick brush at the edge of the parking area.

Her heart drummed in her ears, and she didn't blink. She didn't dare. It felt as if years passed before the bushes swayed a second time.

"There's someone out there," she whispered.

"Stay in the car," Dylan warned. "Let him come to you."

She heard a snapping sound from the rear seat, followed by several metal clicks.

"What are you doing?"

"Gun."

The single syllable hung in the air between them. Several more minutes passed with nothing happening. She was about to explode.

The sound was so faint that she almost missed it. And it came from the opposite side of the building.

"I think I see something," she whispered, her eyes fixed on the far corner of the loading dock.

"Sit tight."

Leaning forward, she stared hard at the shadows. *Is that him?* she wondered silently, trying to determine whether she had actually seen a form in the darkness.

The shadow moved. She was certain of it.

"He's leaving," she cried softly as she tracked the shadow toward the edge of the building.

"Stay put!" Dylan said between gritted teeth.

He's leaving! her mind screamed. Ignoring Dylan and all their well-intentioned plans, Shelby grabbed the satchel of money and yanked open the door.

"Wait!" Dylan yelled from his hiding place.

The money was heavier than she had anticipated, and she nearly stumbled getting out of the car. Without thinking, she ran blindly in the direction of the retreating form.

"Hey!" she yelled as she rounded the front of the car.

The form kept moving.

"I have the money!" she announced as she picked up speed.

The person appeared to look back, then broke into a dead run toward the back of the building. Without giving thought to her action, driven only by her fierce need to be reunited with her child, Shelby followed.

She was only vaguely aware of the sound of footsteps behind her. She watched as the person ahead of her reached the edge of the woods.

"Please!" she called in a raspy, winded voice. "I've got the money!"

She reached the spot where he had disappeared. After just a brief hesitation, Shelby ducked her head and leapt forward. Her front foot settled in the mossy ground just as she felt an explosion of pain in her forehead. There was a flash of bright light, a ringing in her ears, and then nothing.

Chapter Eight

"Shelby?"

She heard his voice above the whooshing of helicopter blades. Opening her eyes, she immediately squinted against a beam of bright light. Her hand came up to shield her eyes. That's when she felt it.

"What?"

"It's a cloth," Dylan answered.

He was so close that she could feel his breath wash over her face.

Slowly she became aware of her surroundings. Her head was resting against something warm and solid. It was a sharp contrast to the damp ground she could feel beneath the rest of her. Her hand moved to the right, and she felt the unmistakable soft ruggedness of denim. She tried to open her eyes again. Dylan's face was the only image she saw.

"Sorry about the light," he offered with a weak smile.

"My head?" she managed.

"Tree branch," he explained, as the wail of a siren echoed in the distance. "I don't think you need stitches, but you've got one hell of a gash."

"Chad?" she asked, leaning to grab a handful of his shirt in order to pull her sluggish body upright.

"Sorry, honey," he said quietly. "No sign of him."

"But we brought the money..." Her voice trailed off, her eyes closed, and she slumped back against him.

His arms wrapped around her, holding her against him as an ambulance skidded onto the lot, spewing gravel.

Two attendants emerged and moved to where Dylan and Shelby sat at the edge of the woods, their bodies illuminated in the glow of the headlights. It was only then that Shelby realized just how many people were gathered around them.

"Who?"

"Other agents," Dylan said, as he relinquished his position to one of the corpsmen. "She was out for about ten minutes."

A young man crouched next to her, shining a small penlight in her eye. It hurt, and she winced in response.

"Sorry," he mumbled. Then, turning to look up at Dylan, he asked, "Any other injuries?"

"She snapped her neck pretty good."

"We'll strap her."

"Strap her?" Shelby yelped. "Strap her to what?"

"Backboard," he explained as the item suddenly appeared by his side, thanks to the other attendant.

"I don't think that's ne—"

"Precaution," he said, interrupting her.

Shelby suffered the indignity of having herself rolled on to the hard board. She was then held in position with a series of leather-and-Velcro straps before being hoisted onto a waiting stretcher. It seemed like overkill, but she had neither the strength nor the inclination to argue. Her mind screamed for answers. *Why hadn't he stayed to collect the ransom? And where was her baby?*

HE FOLLOWED the ambulance in her car. He'd used the time to run it all back in his mind. Dylan had a feeling in his gut. A really bad one. Something wasn't right. It was like he was missing an important fact or bit of information, and he couldn't for the life of him figure out what it was.

He slammed his clenched fist against the steering wheel once before leaving her car in the hourly lot. Luckily, they had taken Shelby to one of the smaller hospitals, so he'd be spared that gory task of sitting among the battered and bloody while she was being examined.

He sucked in a deep breath before passing through the double sliding glass doors. Immediately he was assailed by the scent of disinfectant, poorly masked by some fruity deodorizer. He hated hospitals.

Scanning the area, he found the two ambulance attendants leaning against a tall counter. They were laughing with a little redhead who looked more like a cheerleading captain than a nurse. The observation made him feel old.

"Agent Tanner," the taller of the two corpsmen said.

"Thanks for responding so quickly." Dylan looked to the nameplate pinned above the man's shirt pocket, "Burns."

"No probs," he said with a shrug. "I think she'll be fine once they get her vitals stable."

He felt as if he'd been kicked in the stomach. "Her vitals?"

"Pulse was way up there. So was her pressure."

Dylan mumbled some additional words of thanks and asked the nurse to let him know when the medical team was finished with their evaluation.

He followed the signs to a bank of pay phones. While he waited for the phone to be answered, he rearranged the collection of half-full coffee cups and wondered why the hospital failed to provide a trash can for the waiting area.

"Hello."

"Jay? Dylan."

"How is she?"

"She's still in the ER. I think there's a problem with her blood pressure."

He heard the other man let out a breath before saying, "Understandable, under the circumstances. What about the injury to her head?"

"She took a pretty good hit, but I don't think it did any permanent damage."

"But the guy did show?"

Dylan shifted his weight as he processed the surprise in his boss's voice. "Why wouldn't he have?"

"Right." Jay's laugh seemed forced, almost nervous. "Hang in there for her, make sure she has everything she needs."

"I think the only thing she needs is her son."

He placed the receiver on its cradle and looked down the hall, hoping to catch a glance of Shelby. The corridor was deserted, as was the small waiting area, which was enclosed by a row of dusty plastic palms in large plastic pots.

Selecting a seat on the end of a tattered vinyl sofa, Dylan tried to get his mind off her by staring at the static image on the muted television. He lasted about five minutes, before leaning his head back and closing his eyes.

He remembered vividly what it had felt like to watch her crumple and fall to the ground in the cool, dark woods. If only he'd gotten to her sooner. If only she'd stayed in the car. What, he wondered, had happened to that cautious side of her that had been the beginning of their undoing...?

"DEFINE SLOWLY," he asked, leaning his palms against the smooth surface of the kitchen counter. He felt as if all the breath had been knocked from his body, and he struggled not to let it show.

"Everything's happening so fast, Dylan," she told him, in careful, measured syllables.

"We're not kids, Shelby," he countered, hoping he didn't sound like some sort of groveling high school kid about to be dumped by his girl.

"I know." She smiled then. The action was almost enough to make him forget that he was being brushed off.

"I'm not saying I don't want to see you," she continued. "I just want us to get to know each other a little better before we . . . again."

He liked the fact that her cheeks burned red when she tried to give a name to the intense passion that sizzled between them. "I'm not sorry it happened," he told her.

"I didn't say that I was," she assured him, lowering her eyes.

"Then why are you putting the brakes on?"

She spun gracefully and moved over to the window. She was wearing a skirt that billowed out from her small waist. It might have looked dowdy on another woman, but not Shelby. She had the poise and posture of a dancer. She looked good in everything, but he liked her best in nothing.

"Last night shouldn't have happened."

She wasn't looking at him. Not a good sign.

"Why not?"

"There's too many unresolved issues between us."

"Such as?"

"Ned."

His mood took an immediate trip south. "I'm not asking you to do anything but help us get a dangerous man off the streets."

When she met his eyes, the pain he read in her expression did even more damage to his deteriorating mood.

"I've already told you," she complained. "I don't know about any of the shipments y'all are interested in. I've never seen any guns, or anything remotely lethal."

"But you can get us the information, Shelby. We need someone on the inside."

"Do you know what you're asking me to do?" she wailed, her small fists balled at her sides. "You're asking me to help you build a case against a man who has never been anything other than kind and nurturing to me."

"Really?" he asked as he shifted his feet to shoulder width apart. "Exactly how nurturing is Nichols?"

"For heaven's sake," she groaned as she snatched her jacket and purse off the sofa. "You sound more like a jealous lover than an investigator."

"Maybe that's because I am," he muttered, just as she slammed out the cabin door.

"AGENT TANNER?"

He opened his eyes to find a portly man in a signature white coat staring down at him over the edge of a metal clipboard.

"I'm Tanner."

"Dr. Harrison," he said as he thrust one hand forward.

Rising, Dylan accepted the hand, and was surprised by the firm handshake. Doctors usually treated their hands like their most prized possessions. Especially trauma surgeons, which was the description embroidered beneath the doctor's name on his coat.

"She's resting comfortably now. I'm going to keep her here overnight."

"Is there a problem?"

"All her films were negative, but I'm concerned about her overall health. Her vital signs aren't at all normal for a woman her age. She's extremely upset."

"That's understandable, don't you think?"

The doctor's response was a confused frown.

"She didn't tell you?"

"No."

Dylan spent the next several minutes explaining the crisis that was the underlying cause of Shelby's emotional state. The doctor nodded quietly as he listened, his face impassive. It was obvious that this man was no stranger to horrific events. Dylan envied the man his detachment. It would be so much simpler if he'd never known Shelby. If somehow he could get through all this without tripping over the past.

"I want to alter my orders for her," Harrison said as he scribbled something on the chart. "I think it's advisable that she get some rest."

"What about her head injury?" Dylan queried.

"Minor," the doctor answered. "I'm much more concerned about her emotional state. And now that I fully understand the situation, I can act accordingly."

"Thank you." It was Dylan's turn to offer his hand. "I'll call my superior about arranging for additional security."

Harrison nodded with a resigned sadness. "We have an excellent security staff here, Agent Tanner. I'll instruct the nursing staff to assist you in coordinating your efforts with them."

"They're keeping her overnight," he told Jay a few minutes later. "I'll stay with—"

"You're going home."

"C'mon, Jay."

"Home," came the terse command. "I'll send a unit over now. I want you to leave the moment they arrive."

"But—"

"But nothing," Jay interjected. "Look, Dylan. I know you have an interest in this woman that goes beyond your usual conscientious attention to detail. It's not a problem now, but it could be."

Anger churned in Dylan's stomach. "Meaning?"

"Meaning you need to distance yourself. At least for a while. Take the rest of the night off. Get some sleep. I'll tell the unit you'll be back to relieve them around ten tomorrow morning. Until then, I don't want you anywhere near that hospital. Understood?"

"Yes," he hissed. "Later," he added, just before slamming the phone down.

His reluctance to leave her only increased when he slipped into her darkened hospital room. Soundlessly he moved to the edge of the bed, careful not to disturb her. She looked so frail just lying there, her black hair fanned out against the starched white pillow.

Careful to avoid the wires from the blood-pressure device cuffed around her upper arm, Dylan brushed her bangs away from the small bandage taped to her forehead. Her lashes fluttered, and he actually stopped breathing. Her eyes didn't open.

The silence was disrupted by the automatic inflation of the nylon sleeve. After several seconds, the cuff deflated and a green readout flashed on the monitor above the bed. The numbers were high. Still Shelby didn't move.

Just as he was about to leave the room, Dylan acted on impulse. With utmost care, he leaned forward and brushed a kiss against her lips.

He meant for it to be brief, comforting. It wasn't. He left the room with his fingers pressed to his mouth, her scent still lingering in his mind.

"YOU BLEW IT."

She was dreaming. It had to be a dream. No one actually spoke in that raspy, hoarse whisper.

"You shouldn't have called the cops."

It was a dream, but she could feel the hot breath against her ear. She tried to turn away, but her body wouldn't cooperate. Next she tried to open her eyes, but they were slow in responding. She managed to force her lids open a fraction of an inch. She smelled something. What was it?

"You were supposed to do exactly as I said, Shelby."

"What?" she said through the thickness of her own tongue. She managed to open her eyes a bit farther. The dream was wearing white.

"You'll regret crossing me, Shelby."

Chapter Nine

Dylan took the steps two at a time, a sudden and unexplainable rush of adrenaline fueling his progress. It took a few seconds to work through the series of locks securing his door.

Foolish greeted him by skidding into his legs, nearly knocking him to the floor.

"Hi there," he said as he patted the dog's head. Scooping up the mail, Dylan moved toward the kitchen, battling Foolish all the way.

Flipping on the light, he began to sift through the stack of envelopes, but then his attention was drawn to the table. Or, more accurately, a suspicious-looking paper bag leaning against the bowl of wilting fruit on it.

"What—?" he said as he bent closer to examine the object.

The top of the bag had been twisted, but not secured. He could see inside the bag.

Grabbing a pen from the counter, Dylan tossed aside his mail and used the flat end of the pen to ease open the folds of brown paper.

"Holy hell," he muttered as the contents became clear. Dylan dropped the pen and grabbed the phone.

Jay answered on the first ring.

"I've got another videotape," he said, without preamble.

"You?" Jay asked.

"It was sitting on my kitchen table when I got home."

"How?"

"No kidding, how," Dylan barked. "How in the hell would this guy know to leave a tape here? I haven't exactly been high-profile in this investigation."

"Nichols," Jay responded, without hesitation.

Dylan lowered himself into a chair, his mind working furiously. "This is getting more weird by the minute."

Foolish moved and placed his muzzle against Dylan's thigh. His tail thumped loudly against the tiled floor.

After trading theories with his boss for several minutes, Dylan hung up. He wanted to look around before the forensics guys showed.

The front door showed no signs of tampering. Anger simmered just below the surface as the realization kicked in that his home had been violated by some dirtball.

"Obviously you were a big deterrent," he said to the dog, not bothering to mask his disgust. The dog's ears lifted, and his tail wagged furiously. "I'm criticizing you," he pointed out as he weaved his way through the living room. Foolish followed, apparently undaunted by his master's harsh tone.

The sliding glass door was closed. The lock had been drilled out, a domino-size hole left in the metal framing. Dylan turned to face the dog, hands on his hips, feet braced threateningly apart.

"I don't suppose you barked, or anything?"

Foolish whimpered.

"Dogs are supposed to protect property. Someone comes in here, your job is to bite them, deter crime."

Foolish barked.

The sound was followed by a rapid, insistent knocking on his front door. Automatically Dylan glanced at the clock above the fireplace. Twelve-fifteen. Before he answered the door, he stopped in the hallway and retrieved the small-caliber gun from his ankle strap.

"Yes?"

"Mr. Tanner!" came a painfully familiar, shrilly grating female voice.

He groaned, replaced the gun, and tugged open the door.

Miss Dog Expert was angry. He could tell even before she opened her lipless mouth.

"Your dog is a problem."

He leaned against the wall, watching the spongy pink curlers in her hair bob and wiggle as she spoke.

"I'm sorry if Foolish disturbed you."

"Disturbed me?" Her hands moved to the vicinity of her hips. Dylan wasn't actually sure she had hips. The Expert was given to wearing layer upon layer of clothing, none of it related by color, texture or pattern. He supposed her fashion sense was meant to be eclectic. It was just god-awful, if you asked him.

"That dog barked for a solid hour after you finished fixing your door. I would have thought—"

"When did you hear this, Miss James?"

"Johns."

"Excuse me?"

"My name is Johns, not James," she told him tartly. Her bland brown eyes narrowed significantly. "And it was around eleven-thirty."

"Are you sure?"

Red blotches appeared on her thin neck. "Of course I'm sure, Mr. Tanner. I was trying to watch television, but I couldn't—thanks to you."

"What made you think I was fixing the door?" he asked.

She looked heavenward and let out a loud, annoyed breath. "I saw you."

"You did?"

"I looked over my balcony railing and saw you fiddling with the lock."

"How did you know it was me?"

"Well . . ." she breathed, perplexed. "Who else would have been on your patio at that time of night?"

"Someone breaking in?" he suggested sarcastically.

Her eyes grew wide, and she began shaking her overly large head. "Not in this neighborhood, Mr. Tanner. We don't have a crime problem here."

"Right."

"But we *do* have a problem with your dog."

Dylan fought the urge to slam the door in her face.

"If you don't curb his barking at this stage, it will be impossible to train him properly. Now, take a spray bottle and fill it with one part white vinegar to two parts water . . ."

She droned on for a full five minutes. All he could think of was Foolish, dripping with vinegar, smelling like some sort of decomposing Easter egg. He thanked the Expert and mumbled something about taking her suggestions under advisement. The woman—if she actually was a woman—annoyed him beyond belief.

"Eleven-thirty, huh?" he said to the dog as he moved back to the place where the intruder had gained entry. Foolish attempted to help Dylan examine the hole. His efforts earned him a gentle shove.

"This was a professional job, pal," he said as he ran a pen around the smooth metal edge where the lock had once been. "And it wasn't me," he muttered, adding a few colorful curses for his less-than-observant neighbor.

The forensics team spent more than an hour examining the scene. As expected, there was no trace evidence left behind. That annoying sense that he was missing something nagged at Dylan as sat at the table, passing the videotape from one hand to the other. "Something isn't right."

"No kidding," Jay said as he joined him at the table.

Looking up, Dylan noted that his boss was looking rather ragged. In fact, it was the first time in a long time that he had seen a case get to Jay like this one. Must be the kid, he concluded as he accepted the mug of instant coffee Jay handed him.

"We gonna watch the tape?" Dylan queried.

"I watched it in your living room while you were being printed. It's basically the same."

"So the kid's still alive?" Dylan said, feeling an incredible relief. He was beginning to see Chad strictly as Shelby's son, not Ned's. He couldn't stand the thought of something happening to the little guy. He could pretty much guess what would happen to Shelby if the outcome was bad.

"Why drop one here?"

Jay toyed with a chip in the rim of his cup and shrugged his shoulders. "Maybe Nichols is taunting you."

"If he's in Turkey, how would he know I was working this case?"

"He's managed to orchestrate things flawlessly so far. I mean, he's made sure Shelby receives news of the kid at amazingly regular intervals."

"Then why the low ransom demand?" Dylan dumped some sugar in the coffee and stirred it quickly with one finger.

Jay's expression darkened. His brows drew together in a continuous line. "I can't say. The calls are...unusual."

"SOMEONE WAS HERE," Shelby insisted as soon as Rose had closed the door.

"Of course, lots of people were," Rose stated, patting the perfect curls emanating from her large, teased mass of white blond hair. "Nurses, doctors, orderlies."

"No, someone in white."

Rose slapped her forehead with her palm and clicked her tongue. "That's suspicious. A person dressed in white, roaming around the hospital, must have caused quite a stir."

"I'm telling you—" Shelby let her arms flop down on the hard mattress "—I think it was the kidnapper."

"Shelby, honey," Rose said, comfortingly as she sat on the edge of the bed, "why would the kidnapper come here? They said they gave you something to calm your nerves. You probably just imagined it."

Shaking her head, Shelby persisted. "I know it was him. He was really mad at me for bringing the cops. I think he might hurt Chad because of it."

"If he was going to hurt the baby, he'd have done it by now," Rose stated firmly.

Shelby wondered whether her friend actually believed that. She hoped so.

"I don't know what I'll do if I—"

The phone rang. Shelby reached over and picked up the receiver. "Hello."

"Hi, it's Dylan."

"Hi," she returned hesitantly.

"I'm going to come by and pick you up around—"

Shelby cut in. "Rose is here with me. She's going to give me a lift home."

"Did you get any rest?"

She considered telling him about her visitor, but decided not to. "I slept."

"You okay?" When she didn't respond immediately, he said, "I mean, I know you're not okay. I just wondered how you were doing, what with the botched..." His voice trailed off.

"Has there been any news?" she asked, then held her breath as uncertainty gripped her throat.

"As a matter of fact, there has."

"What?" she demanded, sitting straight up and grabbing Rose's arm as she waited.

"We got another tape."

"Another tape? Is my son all right?"

"He was sleeping."

"Where?"

"It looks like a hotel room."

"Any idea when it was taken?"

"Apparently it was long after the fiasco at the packing plant."

"How could you tell?"

"There was a television on in the background. 'Early News at Ten.'"

"From last night?"

"We've verified it with the station."

"That means he's still alive."

"Of course he is."

Shelby's spirits were much higher after Dylan's call. She had definite cause to be optimistic, and she latched on to that thought in order to retain her sanity.

"Is your smile only about Chad?" Rose asked as Shelby pulled on her dirty clothing from the night before in the minute bathroom.

"What do you mean?"

"C'mon, girl. I know that look. I've had it a time or two myself."

"What look?"

"You and Tanner," Rose explained, in a slow, deliberate tone. "In spite of everything that's happening, the two of you are something to watch."

"I don't know what you're talking about." But she did. Merely being in the same room with him had an odd effect on her. She would never forget her first encounter with the tall, mysterious man....

THE BUZZER FORCED HER from the relative security of her office to the darkened shop. Annoyance quickened her step and straightened her spine.

Pulling aside the small curtain covering the window, she spoke through the painted name of the Charleston Import Company.

"We're closed!" she yelled as she tilted her head to see the face of the late-evening caller.

His eyes were incredible, brilliant, almost too pretty to belong to a man. But they did, and what a man he was. Dressed in a tailored suit the same ebony color as his hair, he had an air of authority that was apparent long before he pressed his identification against the glass.

"I'm Agent Tanner. Alcohol, Tobacco and Firearms."

Shelby unlocked the door and gazed up at the man. "Yes?"

He looked from side to side in a very clandestine fashion before saying, "May I come in, Miss Hunnicutt?"

She eased the door opened and allowed him to enter. A scent, masculine and compelling, clung to him as he brushed past her.

"What can I do for you, Agent Tanner?"

"I'm here in reference to a telephone call you made to the customs office."

She smiled nervously.

"That was just a misunderstanding," she explained. Did that high-pitched voice belong to her? she wondered as a blush warmed her cheeks.

"You didn't call customs?"

"I did, but—" Shelby began hesitantly. "My partner returned the crates to the carrier. They were delivered here by mistake."

"Did you open the crates?"

His tone was her first indication that this was something more than just a bureaucratic field trip.

"I started to open one, which is why I called."

He fished in his suit coat and produced a small notebook and then a pen. She noted that he was left-handed, and wondered why she would notice such an inconsequential detail.

"Can you describe the contents?"

"It looked like gun barrels," she answered, feeling the first stirrings of a problem seep into her mind. "Look," she said as she rubbed her hands together. "I told all this to the customs guy who showed up here to take the crates."

"Can you describe this individual?"

Shelby blinked once, and her eyes grew wider as she gaped at the man. "He looked like a government official."

Her answer earned her a smile from the big man. It was the most attractive, appealing and sexy smile she'd ever seen, and her heart responded by skipping a beat.

"Like me?" he teased, his head tilted to one side.

"Not exactly like you," she admitted, after clearing the lump from her throat.

"Then humor me, Miss Hunnicutt. Describe him."

Shelby lifted her arm with the intention of brushing her hair back off her face. The small act of vanity cost her dearly. Her elbow tapped the edge of a small cloisonné plate, which went crashing to the floor.

Numbly she looked down at the hundreds of shards. Bits of porcelain were glistening in the light filtering down the hallway from her office.

"I'd better get a broom," she mumbled.

"Let me," he said, one large hand coming out and gripping her shoulder.

Small sparks emanated from his touch, singing her skin wherever his squared fingers made contact.

"Don't be silly," she countered with weak smile. She was so embarrassed she wanted to crawl away on her stomach, slither off into obscurity.

"You'll hurt yourself," he insisted.

"Sweeping?"

"No," he said as he tucked his notebook away and placed the pen between his perfectly straight, brilliantly white teeth.

Shelby made a small noise when he scooped her up in his arms and carried her in the direction of the light.

"What do you think you're doing?" she gasped. She was afraid to move, afraid of experiencing any more of his solid body.

"Protecting your feet," he said between clenched teeth.

"My feet?"

"No shoes," he said, as if she were dense. "I'd feel terrible if my visit resulted in an injury. I'm supposed to be one of the good guys."

He placed her gently on top of her desk, but he didn't slide his hands away. His face remained just inches from hers, so close that she could feel his breath. She watched as his eyes roamed over her face, lingering on her slightly parted lips. It was so innocent, and yet so blatant that Shelby gulped in air. Her body grew warm, and she wriggled against him.

He smiled as his hands fell away. His expression was so pleasant, so relaxed, that Shelby wondered if she hadn't imagined those few seconds of interest.

Ignoring her protests, Dylan took a broom and dustpan and cleaned the shards off the floor. She spent the time lecturing herself on decorum.

The first nice-looking man I see in a while, and I go to pieces, *she chided herself as she fanned her face.*

By the time he came back from depositing the remains in the Dumpster, Shelby had managed to compose herself sufficiently. It helped that she had slipped behind her desk, donning her professional persona.

"So," Dylan said as he unbuttoned his jacket and took the seat across from her. "You were going to tell me about the guy who took the shipment."

She again spoke to his tie. "He was young, early twenties or so. His name was Conners or Collins, I think."

One dark brow arched questioningly. "You asked his name?"

Shelby shook her head. "No. He had identification."

"Like this?" he asked, pulling out his badge and passing it across her desk.

As she brought the black leather case toward her, Shelby was struck by two things. First, the wallet had the same pleasant scent as its owner. Second, it carried his body warmth. She swallowed, trying not to think about how hard and warm his body had been when he held her against him.

"Is it?"

"Is it what?" she said, her voice choked.

"Like his?"

She finally got around to looking at the badge and the accompanying identification card. His picture was amazingly flattering for one of those official photographs. It gave his height, weight and date of birth. She read them slowly.

"Well?"

"No," she admitted, after really studying the emblem on the badge and the layout of the card. "It wasn't anything like this."

She looked up to find him nodding, as if he'd expected her answer.

"Is that because he was with customs?" she asked as she handed back the wallet.

His fingertips brushed hers, sending a small jolt through her system.

"Nope." He leaned forward and met her eyes. "It was because he wasn't with customs. They have no record of any of their men coming out to pick up the guns."

Chapter Ten

Shaking off the memories, Shelby pulled on her jeans. "What on earth?" she mumbled as she fingered the crisp white envelope tucked in the front pocket.

Carefully she extracted it. Her eyes were wide as she read the neat block print.

CHAD'S MOM.

Slipping her nail beneath the flap, she broke the seal and peered inside. She braced herself, fearing the unknown.

A small square of paper was folded into the corner. She pulled it out and read.

BE IN YOUR CAR AT 2:00. NO COPS THIS TIME.

"You okay?" Rose hollered through the door.

"Um..." Shelby quickly folded the envelope and the cryptic note and stuffed them in her pocket. "Fine!" she called back. Panic caused her hands to tremble as she ran her fingers through her mussed hair. He *was* here, she thought as she stared at her reflection in the small mirror above the sink. The note also explained the video delivered to Dylan. The kidnapper had provided proof that her son was still fine. She knew at that very instant that she would follow his instructions to the letter. She wasn't going to risk her son's well-being—not again.

It was just before noon when she and Rose emerged from the hospital. The day was gray and dreary, much like her mood. When, she wondered, would this nightmare end?

"I don't mean to harp," Rose said as she slid behind the wheel of her battered car, "but how long do you think it will be before Tanner puts it all together?"

Shelby flicked at the Elvis Presley air freshener dangling from the rearview mirror. "I don't know what you mean."

"Look," Rose said as she angled herself in the seat. "Chad is the spitting image of that man. Obviously you didn't tell him you were pregnant. I'm just wondering how long you think you can keep this charade going."

She leaned back in the seat and closed her eyes. Rose was right. "Once Chad is safely home, there will be no reason for Dylan to stick around."

"Right," Rose muttered as she turned the key in the ignition. "Except he doesn't impress me as the type to just walk away. Not the way he looks at you."

"That was the problem," Shelby admitted in a tired voice.

"I don't know. Man looked at me that way, I'd be tickled pink."

Shelby felt the corners of her mouth twitch. "Dylan and I had chemistry."

"I think you still do," Rose offered.

"Not possible now," Shelby said, surprised by the amount of regret she heard in her own words.

"Why is that?"

She thought for a few minutes before answering. "Dylan and I never really had a relationship."

"But you had a son?" Rose asked. The question wasn't the least bit judgmental, and Shelby was grateful for that.

"Believe it or not, it was only one night."

"That's all it takes."

"Yes," Shelby agreed. "I know."

"There had to be more to it than one night."

"I wanted there to be," Shelby admitted. "There might have been, but we'll never know."

"Did you ever think of giving the guy a shot? I'm telling you, Shelby, the man is smitten."

She cringed. "How smitten do you think he'll be when he finds out Chad is his? You should have heard him when he found out I had a son."

"I heard what he said," Rose told her. "I got the impression he was more upset because he thought Chad was Ned's son."

Rose let it drop, leaving Shelby alone with her guilt and confusion. How would Dylan react if he discovered the truth? Would he understand her reasons? Her fears? Probably not, she decided as they turned into the drive.

She was surprised to find Dylan and Jay huddled in the living room. Several color photographs were scattered across the coffee table in front of them.

When she walked in, Dylan looked up at her, his expression hopeful.

"You look better," he said as he rose. He'd changed into jeans and a short-sleeved silk shirt in a pale gray. The contrast to his dark coloring was flattering—too flattering.

"I feel better," she acknowledged. Absently she felt for the folded envelope and considered sharing the note with them. The words *No Cops* flashed against her brain, and she said nothing.

"Has there been any word?" Rose asked.

Both men shook their heads. Shelby felt a stab of pain in her heart as the realization that her son was still missing banished all other thoughts from her mind.

"What are those?" Shelby asked as she picked up one of the photos. It was a blowup of the woman's hand from the first videotape. Every detail of the ring was visible. It was some sort of signet ring, maybe from an organization.

"So far, Jay hasn't been able to match this to anything," Dylan explained as he moved next to her and tapped the picture. He smelled woodsy and soapy, and it reminded her of the cabin he'd taken her to just after they'd begun the investigation of Ned.

Refusing to allow the memories to haunt her again, Shelby nodded and moved away from the heat of his presence. "What about the new tape? Was it a hotel?"

"They're still going over the tape," Jay answered. "But we're absolutely sure the second tape was made at Waterfront Park."

The first rays of hope filtered through her mind. "If the kidnapper had my baby at the park yesterday, maybe someone will remember them."

"I'm going to work on that today," Dylan said. "The lab boys said that they were probably in the park around lunchtime, based on the shadows."

"I'll go with you. Then we can canvass the area. Hopefully someone saw them," Shelby volunteered.

All three of them looked at her as if she'd just confessed to killing Reverend Martin Luther King.

"Don't you want to stay here?" Rose asked. "What if he should try to make contact?"

Shelby glanced at the clock. It was already after one, and the note was explicit. She needed to be in her car at the appointed time. If she accompanied Dylan, she would be spared the task of trying to think of some plausible excuse to sit in her car, waiting for the contact.

"I...I think I'd like the fresh air."

Dylan was staring at her. Every nerve in her body was aware of his eyes on her, the intense scrutiny as he quietly studied her face. She noted that his expression had darkened.

"Mrs. Porter has a point," Jay interjected. "It might not sit too well with the caller if he tried to reach you."

"The cellular in my car is portable," Shelby explained. "I gave the caller that number in case he needed to reach me while I was out. I'll keep the phone with me while we look for signs of Chad or the woman."

Her reasoning didn't totally convince Jay, judging by the deep furrows etched in his brows. Thankfully, he didn't argue.

"We'd better go," Dylan said as he placed several photos of Chad in his shirt pocket.

Shelby nodded, not trusting her voice.

"I'm going to the Tattoo," Rose said. "Call me there if you need anything."

Shelby smiled at her friend and gave her a hug before preparing to leave. She quickly changed into fresh clothing and ran a brush through her hair, careful to avoid the small bandage on her forehead.

Taking a deep breath, she joined Dylan at the foot of the stairs. She nearly jumped when his fingers splayed across her back as he gently steered her in the direction of the door. Her brain was swimming with conflicting thoughts and emotions. She reminded herself to stay focused on finding Chad. She'd wait for the kidnapper to call and follow instructions, and then she'd have her son back. She clung to that scenario as she slid into the passenger seat.

"We'll park near the customs house and do it street by street," he explained.

"Fine."

She fixed her eyes on the dash, silently willing herself not to think about the fact that she was alone with him. Trying not to focus on the man dominating her peripheral vision. The interior of the car seemed to grow smaller with each passing second—until she was aware of little more than Dylan's broad shoulders, or the sculptured muscles of his upper arms, wrapped in the soft fabric of his shirt.

Shelby closed her eyes, hoping the awareness would fade. It worked. The image her mind produced instantly returned her to the present. She closed her eyes and saw Chad. Only Chad.

"Here," Dylan said, after he pulled into a metered space and handed her one of the pictures.

Shelby ran her fingertip across the image of her son's cheek. Chad liked it when she did that. It always made him laugh, or drool. The tightness in her chest was almost unbearable.

"We'll start on the east side of the street and work our way toward the park."

Shelby disconnected the telephone, slipped in the battery pack and stuck the phone in her purse. She checked her watch. It was a quarter to two.

"Why don't you do the east side, and I'll take the west?"

Dylan's brows arched questioningly.

"It'll save time," she stated, without meeting his eyes. "Can you handle it?"

His voice was so deep, so full of concern, that it almost inspired tears. She didn't want his kindness or his sympathy—not when she felt certain it would eventually turn to contempt.

"I think so," she said, hedging.

"Here's a stack of my cards. Give one to each person you talk to. Tell them to call if they see anything later on."

They had reached the corner. Their shadows were splashed on the walkway in front of them in perfect silhouettes. Shelby checked her watch again—five of two.

"Maybe we should do a couple of these together first."

"No!" she yelled, then instantly regretted it when she noted the surprise and curiosity on his face.

"I can handle it, Dylan. I'm just anxious to get started."

He looked as if he wanted to protest. He hesitated before shrugging his shoulders and crossing the street. Shelby let out a breath she hadn't realized she was holding. Moving quickly, she ducked into the first business.

It was one of those bath-and-fragrance places. She was inundated by the scents of vanilla and lavender. The shop was small, with narrow aisles stacked high with a full variety of soaps and lotions. She frowned when she realized there was no place in the store that would provide privacy. It didn't help matters much when she saw the woman behind the register staring at her with open suspicion.

Shelby smiled at the blue-haired woman and pretended to browse. The heavy scents wafting upward from a bin of carved soaps made her stomach churn. She glanced at her watch and discovered it was a few seconds after the hour. Her anxiety level intensified. "Come on, call," she pleaded as she checked the price on some potpourri.

The woman behind the register followed her every move. Shelby smiled again. The gesture wasn't returned. She moved on to a display of body lotions. Her hand trembled slightly as she feigned interest in one of the bottles. Her toe nervously tapped against the worn floor in time with the agitated beat of her heart. Three more minutes crept by.

Shelby checked the window, searching the opposite side of the street for any sign of Dylan. She was relieved when she saw no sign of the big man. At least she didn't have to worry about him.

"You need help?" the woman asked.

Only it wasn't a question, it was an accusation.

"Just browsing," Shelby returned, as aloofly as possible.

"Let me know if you ne—"

The shrill chirp of the phone sent her digging through her purse. She had the handset to her ear in record time.

"I'm here," she said in a whisper.

"Good job, Shelby."

"I'm sorry about last night. They've been listening to my calls, and I couldn't—"

"Shut up!" came the terse command.

She was instantly silent.

"I told you no cops."

His voice was so angry, so full of menace, that Shelby felt tears well up in her eyes. "No cops this time," she assured him. "How's my baby? Please, tell me he's still all right."

"He's fine," he answered. "So far."

"Please," she begged, turning away from the watchful eye of the shopkeeper. "Please don't hurt him."

"Give me one reason why I shouldn't."

"He's a baby!" she wailed, gripping the phone with both hands. "I'll do whatever you say. Just please, please don't hurt him."

"How do I know you'll follow instructions, Shelby?"

"I will," she promised. "I'll keep the police out of it." The ensuing pause was so long that Shelby feared he might have hung up. "Are you still there?"

"I'm thinking," he growled.

"Just tell me when and where to meet you. I'll bring you the money."

"It won't be that easy."

"What?"

"You have to be punished."

"Taking my son has been punishment enough," she said, without thinking.

"Don't take that tone with me."

"I'm sorry," she said hastily. "I'm just very upset. You can understand that, can't you?"

She heard a noise on the other end. It was the sound of ice tinkling in a glass.

"Of course I understand, Shelby. But that doesn't give you the right to talk down to me."

"I wasn't trying to give you that impression," she insisted.

"Well, you did. And I didn't like it."

She bit her lip, not sure how to respond.

"I think I might know how we can resolve this," he said after a brief silence.

"Anything."

"We'll double the amount. Yes," he said, in an obscenely cheery tone. "One hundred thousand dollars should take care of my inconvenience."

"That's a lot of money." Shelby swallowed. Without the participation of the ATF, she had no earthly idea where she could get her hands on that kind of money.

"Isn't getting your son back worth that to you?"

"Of course," she told him. "But it might take me some time to get that amount together."

"That's fine," he said. She heard him raise a glass to his lips. "I'm a reasonable man, Shelby."

"Then let me talk to Chad."

His laugh was low and completely mirthless. "Not right now."

"Then will you continue to send me tapes?"

"What?"

"The tapes. They are the only thing keeping me sane."

"We need you to stay sane while you get the payoff together," he said after a brief delay. "I'll tell you what, Shelby. I'm feeling generous, so I'll give you forty-eight hours to get it together."

"That's two days!" she nearly shrieked. "I can't stand another two days without Chad!"

"I'll be in touch."

"No!" she whimpered as the line went dead. Fighting both tears and the urge to smash the telephone against the nearest wall, she closed her eyes.

"This isn't a phone booth, honey," the woman announced.

"Sorry," Shelby mumbled as she slipped the portable into her purse. She turned and headed toward the door.

She pushed out of the shop and ran smack into Dylan's solid form. She looked up at him through unshed tears.

"What happened?" he asked as his hands gently gripped her shoulders. The compassion in his voice moved her closer to the edge.

She just shook her head and averted her eyes.

"I don't want to get your hopes up."

Her head whipped up and she noted the small spark in his eyes. "What?" she asked, grabbing handfuls of his shirt.

"I found a guy who thinks he saw Chad and our mystery woman."

Chapter Eleven

Dylan stared down at her, his eyes moving over every inch of her face. Something was wrong. The remnants of tears had left her lashes moist, and the tiny lines around her mouth appeared to have deepened.

It took a few seconds for his brain to register the fact that she was touching him. He could feel the slight tremor in her hands where they rested against his chest. A warm breeze lifted her hair off her shoulders to glisten in the now bright sun. In spite of the circumstances, Dylan was reminded of her subtle beauty.

"I've got what might be our first real break," he told her.

Her lips parted slightly as she sucked in a shocked breath. "Thank God," she managed, in a hoarse, emotional voice.

Allowing his hands to slide down the sleeves of her blouse, Dylan took her hands in his. "Don't get your hopes up until after I check it out," he warned.

"I won't."

But he knew that wasn't the truth. He'd seen the relief bring a glimmer of light into her eyes. Silently he prayed he could find the woman and put an end to this nightmare. Then what? his mind asked. Finding Chad would mean walking out of her life. Again.

He held tightly to her hand as they worked their way toward the Historic District, in the center of Charleston. The streets were thick with tourists and fragrant-smelling street vendor's carts. Dylan noticed little beyond the silky softness of her skin.

"What are we doing?" Shelby asked as Dylan unlatched the ornamental gate of one of the stately homes.

"The guy at the dessert shop said the woman with the baby he thought might be Chad bought a box of those fancy cut-up cakes."

"Petits fours?" she asked.

He responded to her small smile with one of his own. "Whatever," he answered. "He was pretty sure she told him she lived on Market."

"So we're just going to knock on every door until we find this woman?"

"If we have to," he answered as he ushered her into a courtyard garden. "I'll do whatever it takes to find your son."

Shelby gave his hand a small squeeze. It somehow eased her mind to know that Dylan was so committed to finding Chad. It also eased her mind to think they might find Chad before the kidnapper's deadline. The possibility that she might be forced to spend another two days without her baby heightened the knifelike pain in her chest. And, she thought as she ducked under the arm he used to hold opened the gate, she wouldn't have to come up with the money.

Where am I going to get my hands on one hundred thousand dollars? she groaned inwardly.

The first house was structurally just like the Rose Tattoo—a Charleston single house with dual porches and lots of windows. The floor of the lower porch was wide pine plank, covered in layer upon layer of paint.

An oval historical marker was mounted just to the left of the screen door. Beneath that, there was an additional emblem, so tarnished that she couldn't quite make out the inscription.

Dylan yanked open the protesting screen door and lifted the heavy iron knocker several times. The scent of roses floated over from the garden, and she could hear the faint rippling of water from the ornamental pond off in the corner.

"Yes?"

A rotund woman in a domestic's uniform opened the door and eyed them with a mixture of annoyance and curiosity. The annoyance disappeared when Dylan offered his identification.

"Yes, sir. What can I do for you?" She patted the coarse gray hairs that had fallen free from the knot at the nape of her neck.

"We're looking for a missing child," Dylan explained as he handed a picture of Chad to the cooperative woman.

She smiled at the picture. It was an apologetic smile that told Shelby the woman would be of no help. They thanked her and moved on.

For the next several hours, their door-to-door canvass resulted in the interruption of two bridge games, but no sign of Chad. The homes were opulent, standing memorials to Charleston's historic past. She was growing tired of polite dismissals and well-intended wishes for a quick resolution.

"We aren't dead yet," Dylan said as he placed his arm around her shoulder. "Christ," he breathed, his hands closing over her shoulders. "I didn't mean that the way it sounded."

"I know," she said quietly, her head automatically tilted toward his chest. It was a reflexive action, based on her need to be comforted. She tried to convince herself that it didn't matter that it was Dylan's shoulder offering the solace. They walked slowly, without words. For Shelby, it was like taking a much-needed respite. A safe haven from the terrible reality that her baby was in the hands of some stranger. It was getting harder to resist the appeal of having him in her life. Harder to deny that she felt safe whenever he was around.

Their next stop was a large home on a deep corner lot. Again she stood at Dylan's side, reading the historical markers, while he conducted his interview. As her eyes roamed over the various plaques next to the door, something gnawed at her brain. There was something—

"You have?" Dylan was asking in an excited voice.

She looked into the face of the teenage girl who leaned in the doorway, twisting several strands of her strawberry blond hair.

"Looks like him. They just moved in, but I think I've seen her taking him for walks in his buggy."

"Do you know which house?" Dylan asked.

She leaned out, blocking the screen door with her foot and pointed south. "Third house. The green-and-gray one with the carriage stone in the front."

"Thank you," Shelby gushed as she patted the girl's hands.

"No problem," the girl said with a shrug. "Good luck."

Dylan had her by the hand and was nearly dragging her as they sprinted toward the house. Shelby's emotions boiled up to the surface. Was it possible? Was her baby inside that house?

"I want you to stay by the gate," Dylan said.

Shelby stopped suddenly and jerked his arm. "You've lost your mind if you think I'm going to hang in the weeds while you go to the door."

He lifted his sunglasses and glared down at her. His mouth was a thin, determined line. "If the kidnappers are in there, we have to go about this the right way."

"There is no right way," she insisted as they stepped into the shadows of a live oak. "I want my son."

"But I'm assuming you don't want your son hurt."

Shelby's heart stopped for a brief second at the mere thought of Chad suffering. "Of course I don't want him hurt."

"Then we'll do this the right way."

"Which is?"

Dylan's expression softened somewhat. "I'll scope it out. If it looks promising, I'll call for backup."

"That could take hours," she protested.

"But we need to minimize the risks."

Reluctantly Shelby nodded, and she remained hidden by the tree trunk as Dylan strode boldly to the front door. He knocked.

There was no response.

He knocked a second time, with a bit more force.

His efforts were rewarded. A woman answered, wiping her hands on the front of a starched white apron.

"I'm from Charleston Power," Shelby heard Dylan say. "There's been a report of a possible gas leak in the area."

Shelby wondered if the woman would actually fall for that lame story.

"Oh dear!" she said, her hand going to her mouth.

Judging by her accent, Shelby thought she might be from the Midwest. She also looked to be a decade or so beyond her childbearing years.

"Do come in," she said, stepping aside so that Dylan could enter.

The door closed, leaving Shelby alone on the street with her imagination running wild. Could Dylan simply grab the baby and run out? Were there procedures and protocols that might allow that woman to keep Chad after the discovery?

"Does she even have him?" Shelby wondered aloud as the minutes ticked by.

It was more than twenty minutes before Dylan casually emerged from the house. His expression gave her no indication of what had transpired. She did note that the woman in the apron was smiling. She even waved as he retreated through the garden.

"Well?" Shelby asked, grabbing his solid forearm.

Dylan tugged her down the street, nervously glancing over his shoulder until he apparently felt comfortable and stopped.

"Do you have your phone?"

"Of course!" she snapped, reaching into her purse. "Please tell me what you found out."

"It looks like a possibility," he said excitedly.

Shelby welcomed her tears this time. "Oh, thank you," she gushed, before wrapping her arms around him.

"Hold on," he said, wriggling free and placing her at arm's length from him. "I didn't actually see the baby."

"Then how—"

"That's why I need the phone. I need to have Jay run a check on Mrs. Osburne."

"But you said it was promising," she repeated, unwilling to abandon her first real glimmer of hope.

"And it is," he assured her in a soft tone. "The place didn't check out."

"I don't understand."

He took the phone and quickly pressed the buttons for the connection. "Several things were out of whack. Didn't fit."

He held up one finger to keep her quiet while he spoke to Jay. There was a flash of something in his eyes as he spoke to his boss—something Shelby was helpless to decipher. He was kind enough to keep the call brief, but the suspense had her stomach knotted and her palms damp.

"There were bottles in the sink, and a few other indications that there's a kid in the house."

"That woman has to be in her late fifties," Shelby added. That earned her a bright smile from the handsome man. One she felt all the way to her toes.

"She could be a grandmother, but I didn't see any pictures. But that wasn't what bothered me. I couldn't figure out why her house wasn't like yours."

Shelby peered up through her lashes. "We don't exactly share the same tax bracket," she observed dryly. She couldn't even afford the property taxes in this part of Charleston.

"Not like that," he said with a chuckle. "There weren't any of those childproof things you've got all over the place. No plugs in the outlets, no gates near the stairs."

Shelby felt some of her jubilation draining away. "Not everyone takes those precautions."

"But most parents invest in a high chair of some sort."

She thought of the high-tech model that dominated her small kitchen.

"This woman had rigged a dish towel to a chair. Like maybe she was securing the baby for his feedings. Kind of strange, wouldn't you say?"

"Wow," she breathed, allowing herself to rest against a tree. "I can't stand it, Dylan. Let's go back, demand to see the baby."

He was shaking his head, moving closer, so that mere inches separated them. "We have to do this right."

Did he realize what he was asking? she wondered. "But I— She has Chad—"

"We'll get him, Shelby. But we can't just go barging in without doing some sort of background first."

"They didn't mind just barging into my home and stealing my sleeping son."

Dylan felt a pang of intuition. It was a common thing with law-enforcement officials. His sixth sense was itchy. Something wasn't right about all this. He thought back to his brief conversation with Jay. His boss was something less than enthusiastic about this sudden break in the case. From experience, Dylan knew that Jay's instincts were as good as, if not better than, his own. Jay's reluctance remained lodged in his consciousness as he looked down at Shelby's expectant face.

How would he feel if he disappointed her? If they didn't recover her son? The possibility infected his thoughts like a festering wound.

"You've got to prepare yourself," he began slowly.

"I'm trying," she admitted on a breath. "I know this could be another false lead. I just don't want it to be."

"We don't always get what we want in life," he said, not at all sure he was limiting his comments to the plight of little Chad.

A city police cruiser arrived, followed by three more. They parked in front of the Osburne home, blocking the residence. A uniformed officer from the first car came over to them.

"Agent Tanner?"

Dylan nodded and produced his identification.

"Sergeant Gilroy," he said as he offered his hand. "We're waiting on a warrant."

"How long will that take?" Shelby demanded. Both men stared at her.

"This is the mother of the missing boy."

The police sergeant, who looked young and rather thin compared to Dylan, offered a weak smile and touched his finger to the brim of his hat. "Sorry, ma'am."

"How long will it take to get a warrant?" she asked again.

"Not too long," the officer said cautiously. "We'll remain in position until it arrives."

Shelby cursed under her breath. Fury seized her small body, and she gritted her teeth so long that her jaw began to ache.

It was another forty minutes before the warrant was delivered to the scene.

"Finally," she muttered.

"Wait here," Dylan instructed.

"Like hell," she shot back. "If Chad is in there, I'm not going to stand by while a bunch of strange men go tromping in, scaring him worse than he's already been scared."

The two men exchanged a look before Dylan made the determination that she could follow behind them.

Three additional officers joined in the trek to the door. They pulled their nightsticks from their belts as they crept up the stairs. They parted at the door to stand on either side. Shelby was tucked behind Dylan, his large body blocking her view and shielding her from harm.

He knocked.

Nothing.

He knocked again.

Shelby could barely hear the sound of muffled footsteps above the pounding of her heart against her ribs.

Mrs. Osburne appeared at the door, balancing the baby on her left hip.

Chapter Twelve

"Federal agents," Dylan announced, dangling his identification in front of the startled woman. "Gleason," he added, nodding to indicate one of the officers.

The man stepped forward and reached for the child. Mrs. Osburne defensively twisted to the side, preventing the man from touching the wide-eyed child.

"What do you think you're doing?" the woman gasped.

"We're—"

"That's not Chad," Shelby stepped forward to say.

Mrs. Osburne's face registered obvious shock.

"This is Bobby," she said, clutching the child closer to her chest.

There were several awkward seconds when no one, Shelby included, seemed to know what to do next. The woman's initial surprise was rapidly deteriorating into anger. Her faded green eyes sparkled with annoyance as they narrowed to accusatory slits.

"What on earth is this all about?" she demanded, her eyes moving past the small entourage on the porch to take in the scene beyond the garden. Many of her neighbors had followed their curiosity into the street. They manned positions just beyond the barricade of police vehicles.

"Sorry, Mrs. Osburne..." Dylan began.

"Sorry for what?"

"We're investigating the disappearance of a little boy."

The woman's expression softened somewhat. "The son of that woman who owns the bar?"

"Restaurant," Shelby muttered automatically, under her breath. The implication in Mrs. Osburne's tone had put her on the defensive. What did owning the Rose Tattoo have to do with Chad's kidnapping?

"And you thought my nephew was the missing boy?"

"We're checking every lead," Dylan explained.

The baby began to babble happily as he swatted one chubby hand in Dylan's general direction. Dylan surprised her by offering the drooling little boy his finger, which the baby promptly inserted in his mouth.

"I'm sorry we can't help you," Mrs. Osburne said.

Shelby walked away from the house with a very heavy heart. Dylan's warnings about not getting her hopes up hadn't worked. Her ache for her missing son weighted each limp limb.

"It was a shot," he said as he fell into step beside her.

"I know," she managed to choke out.

"We'll find him."

A kaleidoscope of images spun through her mind—Chad's smiling face, the empty crib. Then she remembered the call. She knew then that her best hope of getting Chad back was to follow the kindnapper's instructions. But where was she going to get the money?

"Hey," Dylan said, placing his hand on her shoulder.

She stopped and turned toward him. She could see her reflection in the mirrored lenses of his sunglasses. Looking up at him had the effect of shutting out the rest of the world. Her brain no longer acknowledged the sounds of the city street.

"I'll find him, Shelby," he reiterated softly. "I promise."

She wasn't sure if it was the conviction of his declaration, her tumultuous emotional state, or simply the re-emergence of feelings long buried. It didn't matter, really. She leaned into him, without care or thought for the consequences. His body was large and warm, his arms were comforting, protective. Dylan welcomed her, stroking her hair as she rested her cheek against the solidity of his broad chest.

Drinking in the scent of him, she closed her eyes and allowed her tears to flow freely. He responded by whispering compassionate words against her ear. She cried until the tears stopped of their own accord. When she lifted her head, she felt drained and exhausted, but that wasn't the most telling emotion.

His sunglasses were gone. She found him looking down at her with raw emotion in his eyes. She should have pulled back, out of his arms. She should have apologized and made some distancing excuse for stupidly turning to him for comfort. But all rational thoughts evaporated as his hands slowly glided over her shoulders until they gently cupped her face.

She felt the calluses on his palms as his thumbs made small circles against her face, erasing the remnants of her tears. He bent forward, until his breath washed over her face in soothing waves. The pulse at her throat fluttered as his fingers fanned over her skin. Her head tipped back as her lips parted ever so slightly. Shelby hovered on the precipice of indecision. Rational thought eluded her as she watched his eyes drop to her mouth. Her breath stilled in her throat when he looked at her like that.

Although she'd expected the contact, it still sparked a thousand fires in her motionless body. His mouth was gentle, tentative, the kiss little more than a whisper of a touch. When it was over, he didn't lift his head. Instead, he laced his fingers behind her neck and leaned his forehead against hers. She could hear his uneven intake of breath.

"I'm not going to say I'm sorry," he said. But he was. He was sorry time and circumstances made it impossible for him to kiss her the way he wanted to. For now, he knew, he would have to settle for offering comfort.

"It was nothing," she told him in a small voice.

Reluctantly Dylan allowed her to step away from him, though he managed to retain his grasp on her hand. It felt small, and he thought he detected a slight tremor as his fingers entwined with hers.

"Let's call it a day," he suggested as he tugged her in the direction of the car.

He was content to walk in silence with her at his side. He liked just having her with him again. He was willing to take whatever crumbs she might toss in his direction. His stomach knotted as he realized what was happening. It was like stepping back in time. Back to when he'd first met her, first fallen in love with her.

"Dylan, look!"

He was reaching to unlock the door of her car when his attention was directed to the rear seat. He froze.

Mumbling a string of expletives under his breath, he kicked the tire with enough force to rock the car. A videotape was resting in plain view, in her baby's car seat. The perversity of the scene, and its effect on Shelby, made every muscle in his body tense with a subtle, barely controlled fury.

"We should call and have the car dusted," he explained. When she looked up at him with those sad blue eyes, he almost abandoned procedure. "It's not worth risking the possibility of getting a handle on this guy," he said, in response to her unasked question.

Jay arranged for them to wait at the Rose Tattoo while the car and the video were being tagged, taped and photographed. They arrived just as the early dinner crowd began to fill the tables on the patio. He was impressed by the business.

This place, with its hanging baskets and trendy menu offerings, was a far cry from the overpriced knickknack shop she'd run with Nichols. The mere thought of that slimeball made him grit his teeth. He wondered where Nichols was at that very moment, and whether he knew what he was doing to Shelby.

"Let's go upstairs," she said as they weaved their way through the bar area.

The sound of Elvis singing gospel tunes filtered through the din of conversation. The small blond waitress, Tory, emerged from the kitchen area, balancing a dish-laden tray slightly above her head.

He almost missed the flash of fear he saw cross her face when she saw Shelby. Dylan filed that away, along with some other things that were beginning to challenge his initial impression of the abduction.

"How are you doing?" Tory asked, stopping long enough to give Shelby's arm a squeeze.

"Hanging in there."

"Any leads?" she asked, giving Dylan only a brief moment's attention.

He shook his head and watched as she began to buckle beneath the weight of the tray.

"I'm so sorry," Tory said, before going on about her duties.

This scenario was played out as each of the employees stepped forward for an update and to offer heartfelt words of encouragement.

"You need to buy a few new records for your juke-box," he said as soon as they reached her office.

Her smile was genuine. "Rose would kill me. We only play the King."

"Why?" Dylan asked as he sat on the edge of her desk. Shelby seemed more relaxed now, as she slid into the chair.

"Rose is a *real* Elvis freak. She even makes a pilgrim-age to Graceland each year on his birthday. She's a hard-core fan. You should see her house. It's a shrine."

He whistled and chuckled at the image. Rose Porter was a character. He didn't share Jay's reservations about the woman.

"You didn't know anything about her husband or her kids?" Dylan asked.

She leaned back and locked her hands behind her head. He tried not to notice how the action caused her sweater to hug every curve of her body. It was a struggle.

"Not really."

"Meaning?"

She shrugged and said, "She was really helpful when Chad was born. I never questioned her, but she knew an awful lot about newborns."

He realized that his image of Shelby was expanding. The knowledge that she was a mother had been a shock. And he still wasn't completely comfortable with the fact that she had this tie to Nichols.

"I'm sure it was nice having someone around when Chad was born."

Her movements became still, forced. She couldn't meet his eyes. He wondered at the reason for her reaction. It was like watching a door close and hearing the bolt slide into place.

"Tell me about the guy behind the bar."

"Josh?"

He nodded as he plucked a pen from its holder and began to twirl it in hand.

"Josh came with the place. Same as Tory."

"You bought people?" he asked, teasingly.

Some of the small tension lines around her mouth appeared to ease. "They worked here when Rose originally bought the place."

"So you and Rose didn't start this together?"

"I invested the money that came from selling my interest to Ned."

The mere mention of the guy's name produced a sour taste in Dylan's mouth. He was sure he was frowning when he asked, "Why would Nichols let you buy out, knowing you were—"

Her eyes met his. There was definite challenge on their brilliant blue depths. "Ned didn't *let* me do anything."

"Then why the split? Why did you leave?"

Having risen from the chair, she offered him her back as she peered out the window. "Ned was furious with me when he found out I had been meeting with you."

"He should have been. We should have nailed that slimeball." His words echoed in the still room.

"It was complicated, Dylan."

"Your business partner was—and still is—an arms dealer."

He noticed a definite stiffening of her spine, but couldn't seem to contain himself on the issue of Nichols. "Okay," he began, as his blood pressure went up a notch or two. "Forget his criminal shortcomings. I don't understand why he'd let you walk out of his life when you were carrying his child.''

"For the last time—" she turned, her eyes narrowed and fixed "—it's complicated and personal, Dylan. And not open for discussion. All right?"

Hell, no! his mind screamed. He couldn't stand to let go of it, but he had no choice. She stood her ground, her arms folded in front of her. He could see the rapid rise and fall of her chest as she took each annoyed breath.

"Dylan?"

"Yep?"

"I don't want us to discuss Ned every time we're together."

That small crack in the wall she'd put up against him was all he needed. He moved next to her, taking her small hands in his. She smelled faintly of wildflowers, and looked as if the weight of the whole world rested upon her slender shoulders. Arguing about Nichols had destroyed their budding relationship once before.

"Sorry," he said, lifting her hands to his lips.

Their eyes remained locked as he brushed his lips across the back of each hand in turn.

"You shouldn't do that," she said in a near whisper.

"Why?" he asked against her skin.

"You know why."

"The only thing I know," he said as he turned her hands and placed kisses in her palms, "is that I have a hard time keeping my hands to myself when you're around."

"We knew that," she admitted, tugging her hands from his. Sidestepping him, she moved to the relative safety of her desk.

"Then why didn't it work?"

He couldn't see her face, but he heard her heavy sigh.

"It just didn't, Dylan. There's no need to do a post-mortem."

He didn't agree, but he let it pass—for now.

"Why do you think he's sending the tapes?" she asked.

Dylan sauntered back to the desk and perched on the edge. "Good question."

"Do kidnappers usually send videos?"

"Sometimes. Sometimes they send other stuff."

"How did he know you and your men were there last night?"

Dylan's foot tapped nervously against the floor. "There was a mix-up on the far side of the plant."

"What?" she fairly shrieked.

"A couple of the men were out of position."

"And just what does that mean?" she demanded, getting to her feet.

He nearly winced at the sharp edge to her voice. "There was a miscommunication."

"You're beating around the bush," she said accusingly.

"Two guys moved out of position at the perimeter," he explained. It sounded just as lame as when Jay had told him. "They apparently misunderstood their instructions."

"Good Lord!" she cried, falling back into the chair, holding her head in her hands. "You mean I could have gotten my son back last night, but you guys screwed up?"

He raked his hands through his hair, trying to think of something to say. "It was unfortunate."

"Unfortunate?" she parroted. "Why wasn't I told about this last night?"

"You were in no condition."

"How could this have happened?" She rubbed her eyes, then began a slow massage of her temples.

Jay wouldn't be too happy to hear that he had shared this bit of information with her.

"Mistakes happen, Shelby. Two of our men left their positions prematurely."

She looked up at him, her eyes wide with disbelief. Her expression worked like a machete, slicing its way through his gut.

"It was regrettable, Shelby. But we'll get him. Hell," he said as he moved next to her. Swiveling her chair, Dylan knelt in front of her, his hands resting on the tops of her thighs. "We've got a lead on Nichols in Turkey. As soon as he's questioned, I'm sure we'll be—"

"Ned isn't behind this!" Shelby wailed, tossing his hands aside as if his touch appalled her.

"Then give me something else," he nearly pleaded. "He's the only enemy you've got."

"He isn't my enemy," she insisted. "He would never do anything like this to me."

"Who besides Ned Nichols knows so damned much about you?"

"What?"

He jumped to his feet and began pacing, trying to allow his muddled thoughts to solidify.

"Dylan?" she prompted. "What are you talking about?"

"Think, Shelby. This guy knows your home, your place of business. He seems to always be one step ahead of us. Obviously he's no stranger to your daily routine."

Her hand clutched her throat as she absorbed his words. "You're saying it has to be someone I know?"

"And who do you know, besides Nichols, who would be capable of something as low as snatching your son?"

"This is crazy."

"But it's not," Dylan insisted, moving back to capture her face in his hands. "There's too many aspects of this that don't fit the typical kidnapping."

"What does Jay think?"

Dylan took a breath and exhaled slowly. "He is focusing his attention on Nichols."

"And you're not?"

His fingers brushed a few strands of her silky hair away from her upturned face. "I'm leaning toward Nichols. But I'm not closed-minded."

"That's comforting?"

"I'll admit I'm having some trouble fitting Nichols into every aspect of the case."

She reached up, and he felt her fingers close around his wrist. Her hand was as warm as the small smile she offered. He could almost see the thoughts churning through her mind. Her expression stilled and grew serious, almost frightened.

"If we rule out Ned—"

"I didn't say I was willing to go that far."

She pursed her lips. "For the sake of argument?"

"Fine."

"If it isn't Ned, then how would a total stranger know so much about me?"

He hesitated, trained those cool gray-blue eyes on her and said, "What if it isn't a stranger?"

Chapter Thirteen

"Tell me again why we're doing this," Rose muttered as she inserted her key in the lock.

"I need to make a call, and I want it to be private."

"Does this have something to do with Chad?" Rose asked, one brown arched high on her forehead.

Shelby didn't meet her friend's eyes. "I just wanted to get away from Dylan."

Rose flipped a switch on the wall, flooding the small house with yellowish light. A life-size cardboard cutout of Elvis Presley greeted Shelby as she stepped into the cramped living room. The decor conveyed both the taste and the personality of its owner. Every conceivable inch of the room was home to some form of memorabilia. There were street signs, movie posters, coffee mugs, ashtrays. But Shelby's favorite was the Plexiglas-enclosed item resting next to the hound-dog-shaped telephone. An engraved brass plate mounted on the glass announced that the whitish, half-moon-shaped item was one of the King's fingernails. It was so disgusting that it inspired a certain amount of morbid amusement.

"You didn't seem to mind having Dylan around earlier," Rose said.

"What are you talking about?"

Leaning forward through the small space that separated the kitchen from the living room, Rose said, "I saw you two in the office. I don't think he was fingerprinting you with his lips."

A guilty warmth spilled on to her cheeks. "I wasn't—"

"Don't feel the need to explain yourself," Rose interjected. She flipped her hand in the air, causing the vast array of bracelets on her arm to clang and jingle. "Dylan seems like a pretty okay guy. Lord knows he's about as cute as they come." Rose pulled a can of coffee from the freezer compartment. "All that dark hair, and that sorta sexy half smile. Kinda reminds me of the King when he was in *Love Me Tender.* That was the one where he died at the end." Rose's voice took on a wistful quality. "Yes. Your Dylan has that same look."

"He isn't mine," Shelby insisted. "I just hope this ordeal ends soon, so I won't have to be around him anymore."

"Coulda fooled me."

"Rose . . ." Shelby groaned.

"Well." Rose marched out of the kitchen, her stiletto heels muted by the thick pile carpeting. "Who are you kidding? Not me." Rose loomed over her, brandishing a chrome coffee scoop. "Once your initial shock wore off, you warmed right up to that man."

"Warmed up to him?" Shelby snorted. "I've done nothing of the kind. I'm in a very precarious position. I can't very well tell him to take a hike. Not until I've gotten my son back."

The lines at the corners of Rose's eyes deepened. "I know you're worried sick about the baby, but I also see what's going on between the two of you."

"Now you are being ridiculous."

"Really?" Rose said, her tone taunting. "Honey, you can't be in the same room with that man without your eyes following his every move."

"That's silly."

"Now, I can't say as I blame you. I think he's right easy on the eyes myself."

"Rose!" Shelby whined. "I'm not interested in Dylan like that."

"If you're breathing, you're interested. He's too fine a man to go unnoticed."

"Maybe for you," Shelby mumbled, primly folding her hands in her lap. "But I'm immune."

Rose snorted. "And the King really is alive and living in Hoboken."

Shelby rolled her eyes. "I *am*."

"No," Rose said, her tone somewhat less forceful. "You backed yourself into a corner by not telling that man the truth."

"I did the only rational thing I could," Shelby replied defensively.

Rose sat on the sofa next to Shelby, and placed one heavily jeweled hand on the fabric between them. "Secrets as big as yours always come back to haunt you." Her eyes dropped to the sofa, and she began to trace the outline of the leopard-spot print. "Take me, for example. Look at all the dirt they dug up on me in such a short time."

"I'm really sorry about that," Shelby told her.

Rose shook her head. "Doesn't matter. The point is, a secret like the one you're hiding is bound to blow up in your face."

"I won't let it. As soon as Chad is safely back home, Dylan will be out of my life."

Rose's mouth curved downward. "I think you're deluding yourself, Shelby. How do you expect that man to walk away, when the two of you are joined at the lips?"

"We haven't really kissed," she insisted. "Dylan is only trying to comfort me."

"I want to offer you comfort, too, but I sure as hell don't plan on kissing you."

On that note, Rose went into the bedroom, in order for Shelby to use the phone in private. *Great,* Shelby thought as she dug in her bag for her address book. As if things weren't already complicated enough, now Rose wanted her to reassess the situation.

"It won't happen," she said as she waited for the international operator. "Dylan and I have chemistry. But we have nothing in common. It could never work with us. We're too different. I knew that when I broke up with him. And nothing's changed." *Unless you count Chad,* her mind added.

Reading off the code on her calling card, Shelby asked for a specific number and listened for the series of clicks and static as the connections of modern technology warred with primitive electronics. Shelby nervously twisted several strands of her hair around her finger.

"Come on," she pleaded.

Her patience was rewarded when a high-pitched voice recited the name of the hotel.

"Ned Nichols, please."

"Nick?"

"Nichols," she repeated slowly.

She allowed her eyes to roam around the room. She could trace the life and career of Elvis from his early childhood to the final months of his life, thanks to the photos, news clippings and other items framed, mounted or otherwise displayed on every inch of wall space. She couldn't imagine being so committed to anything. Especially a total stranger.

"No Nick," the voice said.

"Not Nick," she just about screamed into the receiver. "Nichols. Ned Nichols. Charleston, South Carolina."

"Nichols."

She cursed and fiddled with the orange plastic tail on the base portion of the novelty phone.

"Hello?"

"Ned?" she breathed into the receiver.

"I'm sorry. This is Mr. Chan. I'm with the hotel. I understand you are trying to reach one of our guests?"

"Yes," she said, adding words of gratitude to be rid of the language barrier. "I'm looking for Mr. Ned Nichols."

"Ahh... Mr. Nichols."

Good, she thought. "Yes, Ned. It's very important that I talk to him."

"I'm afraid that won't be possible."

"He isn't there?" she cried, feeling the cool finger of panic tickle her voice.

"Not at present," Mr. Chan answered. "He's expected later this morning."

Shelby stared at the phone for a long time after hanging up, mentally weighing her options. There weren't any, she acknowledged with a sigh.

"Finished?" Rose asked as she stuck her head into the room.

"Yep."

"What's all this about?" her friend queried as she placed two mugs of steaming coffee on the table. "You aren't doing something stupid, are you?"

She couldn't meet her friend's eyes. "Of course not."

DYLAN PARKED in the alley, and made his way to the back door. Keith answered his knock.

"Yes?"

"I need to talk to Tory Conway," he stated.

Keith made no move to step away from the door. "She's busy."

"Yeah, well," Dylan muttered as he squeezed past the man, "I'm busy, too. I'm trying to find Shelby's son."

The kitchen was in a state of chaos. Pots and pans littered the counters; the equipment was in pieces, and various items were soaking in three of the four large sinks. The room smelled of herbs and stale grease, and still held the heat of the now quiet ovens.

"Where is she?"

Keith's eyes narrowed in a mute challenge.

"Look," Dylan said, in his most official voice, "don't jerk my chain, pal. I'm in no mood for it."

Keith shrugged and tossed his head in the direction of the dining area. He then shuffled off to tend to the items in the sink.

The sound of clanging steel followed him into the dimly lit room. He spotted Tory out on the porch, sitting at a small table, chasing food with a fork.

"Miss Conway?"

She jumped at the sound of his voice, and her light eyes regarded him warily as he turned the chair and fell in next to her.

He could almost sense Shelby out here on this porch. She was the kind of woman designed for soft breezes and sunny afternoons. It was easy to summon an image of her seated on one of the rattan swings, her shapely legs dangling, her silky hair lifted off her long neck.

"Tanner, right?" Tory asked, averting her eyes.

"Dylan," he said. "I need to ask you a few questions about Chad."

"Why me?"

"Just a formality," he answered. He schooled his tone to remain bland, not to react to the nervous quaver in her voice.

She was a petite woman who looked much younger than her mid-twenties. Her light hair, dark tan and curvaceous build made him think of a California poster girl.

"So, what do you want to know?"

She still wasn't making eye contact.

"How long have you worked here?"

"About seven years."

He opted to listen, rather than take notes. He suspected any attempt to record the conversation would only heighten the young woman's anxiety. "Like it?"

She stabbed at a chunk of chicken, but made no move to place the food in her mouth.

"Of course I like it," she told him. "I make decent tips, and my days are free."

"To do what?"

"School."

"You're in college?"

"Graduate school. But I've taken this quarter off."

He noted that some of her tension had abated. "In what area?"

"Historic preservation," she said with a smile.

That small act did wonders for her. Tory was an attractive young woman when she smiled. But not as attractive as Shelby, he thought.

"I'm working on a doctorate. My area of concentration is architectural preservation."

"Sounds interesting," he lied. "Where do you go to school?"

He whistled when she named a prestigious, expensive and exclusive private college on the outskirts of Charleston. "You need those good tips. Tuition alone must run you around twenty grand a year."

"Seventeen-five," she said in a soft voice.

"That's a piece of change."

"Yes," she said, dropping her fork. She made a small sound when the utensil banged against the china. "I'm... um... I'm on a partial scholarship. So that helps."

"And you make up the rest working here?"

"Mostly."

"Married?"

She gave a nervous laugh. "No."

"Boyfriend?"

Gathering up the remnants of her meal, Tory rose, but remained at the edge of the table.

"What does this have to do with Chad being kidnapped?"

"Routine," he said, watching her intently. "We need to know about the people in Shelby's life."

"I don't have a boyfriend," she said quickly. A devilish light sparkled in her eyes. "In fact, I haven't even had a date in recent months."

"I know the feeling," Dylan said under his breath.

"You?"

He actually felt his cheeks grow warm as a result of her question. "Anyway," he said, clearing his throat. "Have you noticed anyone hanging around here? Maybe asking about Shelby or the baby?"

Tory shook her head sadly. "Shelby keeps pretty much to herself. I mean, she's polite, but she usually stays in her office unless we have some sort of disaster. Rose, on the other hand, thinks nothing of busing a table or mixing a drink."

"Speaking of drinks, what can you tell me about Josh?"

"Wow," Tory said as she scratched her head. "Great bartender. Fast. And he's nice, but a real trawler."

"Trawler?"

"Contrary to current advice, Josh has a thing for one-night stands. He rarely leaves here without his nightly trophy."

"Sounds like a real prince."

Tory flipped her bangs back away from her face. "He's not evil, he's just not real big on responsible adult relationships, or the concept of commitment."

"Do I detect a note of bitterness?"

Tory snickered. "He's nice-looking, and we went out a couple of times. Josh was a gentleman, but it nearly killed him in the process. I think he's uncomfortable with women with IQs in three digits."

"How's he feel about working for two women?"

Her brows drew together as she appeared to mull over the question. "I never gave it much thought. He's never said anything nasty about Shelby. Only Rose."

"He has a problem with Rose?"

"Rose can be blunt. Josh doesn't take it well when someone points out his shortcomings. Rose delights in taking him down a peg or two."

Dylan thanked Tory, and walked to his car. All of this was accomplished under the watchful eye of Keith. He drove back to his apartment, with his mind replaying the interview.

"Something doesn't fit," he told Foolish. "There's something I'm not seeing."

HE ARRIVED early in the morning, the videotape tucked under his arm. Shelby tracked his movements from the relative safety of her bedroom. He was wearing jeans and a short-sleeved white shirt. He walked with such authority, yet each lithe movement was relaxed, fluid and confident. She loved to watch him move.

She wondered if Chad would inherit that confident walk. The thought brought the familiar pain to her chest. "He's okay," she said aloud. "Just think about the videotapes."

When Dylan knocked on the door, Shelby felt her heart flutter in her chest. It was silly, futile, but she couldn't seem to stop herself from reacting to this man.

"How are you?"

"Holding up," she lied. She still hadn't reached Ned. The money was weighing heavily on her mind.

"Jay will be here in a little while," he told her as he brushed past her.

The scent of soap and his cologne was incredibly comforting as his massive form filled the small vestibule. He was smiling down at her, his eyes searching her face.

"I can't get over how well you're doing," he said as his fingers closed around the bared flesh of her upper arms.

"I'm not doing well," she told him in a shy voice. "I'm operating on autopilot, and constantly reminding myself that I have to stay rational for Chad's sake." *But I'd love it if you held me,* she added silently.

"He's a lucky little boy," Dylan remarked as their eyes met.

"Yes," she managed to say as she backed away from his disturbing closeness. "Chad and I are lucky to have each other."

An awkward silence ensued. She was aware of everything. His size, his smile, the intensity of those eyes. It caused every nerve ending in her body to take on a life of its own.

"Do I smell coffee?"

"Yes," Shelby gushed, grateful to have something to occupy her mind besides him. "I'll get you some."

She all but ran into the kitchen, chased by the ghosts of her guilty past. "How can I be glad to see him?" she asked as she got cups down from one of the cabinets. It was turning into a dangerous and potentially disastrous situation. One she knew she would have to deal with.

"But not right this instant," she whispered as she carried the mugs into the living room.

Dylan was seated on the sofa, his legs crossed at the knee. He looked relaxed, and quite comfortable. His eyes were her only indication of what he really felt. She saw a sadness mingling with frustration when she met his pointed stare.

"I'm flattered," he said, his deep voice resonating through the still house.

Nervously Shelby took the seat at the opposite end of the couch, allowing as much space as possible between them. "Flattered?"

"You remembered," he said, nodding in the direction of the coffee cup. "Hot and black."

"I guess I did," she admitted, with a small smile.

"I like that."

"Don't make too much out of it," she warned, trying to inject some lightness into her tone.

Dylan slid across the sofa until mere inches separated them. "I'm trying not to," he said quietly. His hand came up, and he captured a lock of her hair between two of his fingers. He silently studied the dark strands, his expression clouded and indecipherable.

"I never thought I'd see you again," he continued, his voice low, almost seductive.

"Let's not do this," she said, swallowing.

"I just don't understand what happened, Shelby. It was like everything was fine one minute, and then you gave me my walking papers out of nowhere."

"Please, Dylan," she pleaded, cowering in the small space he'd allowed. "It just didn't work out."

"But I don't know why."

The sincerity in his voice worked like a vise on her throat. The lump of emotion threatened to strangle her as the moments of silence dragged on.

"Just tell me why, and I'll leave it alone."

Closing her eyes, Shelby actually entertained the thought of telling him the truth. Getting it all out in the open. *Then what?* her voice of reason asked. The answer was all too clear. She had no way to gauge his reaction. But she wasn't going to risk it, not when Chad's welfare still hung in the balance.

"I told you that night," she stated in a flat tone. Raw nerves propelled her from the sofa. She carefully placed herself on the opposite side of the table, and tried to ignore the desperation in his eyes. "We don't have anything in common. We want different things."

"We never talked about what we wanted," he countered, his voice rising a notch.

"That was one of the problems. Our relationship was too...passionate."

"Worse things can happen between two people, Shelby."

"But there's more to life than sex."

He jumped to his feet and caught her by the arms before she had a chance to react. As he pulled her closer, she encountered the solid outline of his body. His expression was pleading, his mouth little more than a taut line.

"It was more than sex, Shelby. And I think you know that."

Chapter Fourteen

"We made a mistake early on," Shelby said as she swept her coffee cup off the table. The now lukewarm liquid splattered on the table.

They grabbed napkins and went for the spill in unison. Dylan intentionally allowed his hand to brush hers as his eyes remained fixed on her face, watching. He could tell from her expression that the contact was disturbing, and he was fairly certain he wasn't filtering the observation through his ego. That was the kick of all this, he thought as he dabbed at the coffee. The signals were still there. She was too nervous, and he'd caught her looking at him more than once during the past few days. Her actions and her words didn't mesh. The knowledge only served to sour his mood.

"Don't pout," she told him.

The sound of her soft voice brought him back to the present. "I'm not pouting."

"Then don't frown."

Her eyes were the color of deep, still water. Her lashes were thick and feathery. While he admired her strength, Dylan found her vulnerabilities most appealing. This woman inspired a primitive need to protect, to comfort.

"What would you like me to do?" he asked with a sigh.

Her shoulders lifted in a shrug. The action revealed the slender curves of her body, forcing him to look away. A definite sense of self-loathing enveloped him as he silently berated himself for thinking such thoughts. He needed to get a grip.

"I just don't feel up to sparring with you, Dylan. I can't think of anything right now but the welfare of my baby." Her voice was low, almost pleading.

"Deal," he said, forcing a smile to his lips. He hesitated before speaking again. "I went to see Tory last night."

Her head cocked to one side. "She's very attractive."

"I suppose," he agreed.

"Most men think so." Her words came out in a rush.

Was this a spark of jealousy? he wondered, hopeful. "She's definitely an asset to your business."

"She's a competent waitress."

He smiled.

"What?" She drew her hands up to rest them against her small hips.

"Competent?" he parroted. "Isn't that a little cold?"

He liked the small stain of red on her high cheekbones. Jealousy was looking more and more like a possibility.

"Okay." Shelby lifted her chin regally and met his eyes. "She's the best waitress in all of Charleston."

Dylan's chuckle didn't sit too well with her. Shelby's eyes narrowed, and her lips pulled into a taunting smirk.

Dylan relaxed against the sofa, his eyes never leaving her face. "Tory definitely has a lot on the ball."

"You actually noticed her brain?" Shelby asked, feigning great surprise.

"Right after I checked out her incredible body. Does she work out?" He tried to make the last remark sound conversational. He was glad to see his teasing was relaxing her a little. God knew she needed a break from the strain.

"No. She's just one of *those* women."

"Those?"

She tossed her hands in the air, her face contorted with exasperation. "She eats like a horse and has never once set foot in a gym."

"A horse, huh?"

"Dylan?" she said. "If you want inside information on one of my employees, I suggest you put your request in writing."

His laughter chased her into the kitchen. Her hand was still shaking as she poured herself another cup of coffee. Turning, she leaned against the counter and gripped the steaming mug in both hands.

Damn him, she thought. He'd been provoking her, and, like a fool, she'd gone for the bait. It would never have happened if he hadn't appeared on her doorstep looking like *that.* She tried to tell herself it was just because she was so exhausted.

Dylan had that unmade-bed, casual-sensuality look about him that left her weak in the knees. Every touch, every look, inspired a definite tingling sensation that began in the pit of her stomach and branched outward until she was consumed with her own awareness of him. The man was as annoying as he was exciting.

And he's the father of your child, her little voice of reason reminded. She felt her whole being slump beneath the weight of her secret. Her mind instantly produced one of the images from the last video. She clung to the memory of her son's happy face. Chad had to be okay. There would be time enough for her to sort through her feelings for Dylan. Right now, she had more pressing things on her mind. One hundred thousand of them.

"Morning."

She jumped at the sound of Jay's voice. Turning, she offered a weak smile. Only then did she realize that she had again sloshed coffee.

"She seems to have developed a drinking problem," Dylan said from over the other man's shoulder.

"Cute," she muttered as she surveyed the damage. Depositing the cup in the sink, she pulled the now splattered fabric of her blouse between two fingers. "I'll just run up and change," she said.

Jay backed out of the doorway. Dylan wasn't quite as generous. He planted his large body to one side, making it impossible for her to pass without brushing against him. Shelby held her breath and willed herself not to think about the solidness of his thighs, the rigidness of his taut stomach.

The transferred heat of his body still warmed her skin long after she'd shed her blouse. The annoying hammer of her pulse pounded as she surveyed the contents of her closet. After settling on a pale gray sundress, Shelby ran a brush through the unruly mass of her dark hair. Her eyes fixed on the phone, then the clock on the nightstand. She was running out of time.

Taking a seat on the edge of the bed, Shelby reached tentatively for the phone. After a few seconds of internal debate, she dialed the series of numbers and gave her instructions to the international operator.

"Come on," she whispered as she listened to the static on the other end. She forced herself not to think about the possibility that her outgoing calls were being taped. Her body gave an involuntary shudder at the mere thought of Dylan and Jay discovering what she was trying to do.

"Hello."

"Ned. It's Shelby."

Her breathy whisper was greeted by silence.

"Are you there?"

"Yes."

"I need help."

"I know."

"You know?" she asked.

"I've just spent the past three hours being interrogated by two goons from the State Department."

Shelby let out a long breath, and her fingers nervously twisted through the plastic cord of the phone. "I need money."

After what sounded like a snort, he said, "From the kidnapper?"

"I know you didn't take my son."

"Really?"

His voice was strained, angry, much as it had been on that day when he discovered her involvement with Dylan.

"I didn't get that impression when I was dragged out of bed and through the streets of Istanbul."

"I'm really sorry that happened."

"I'm sure you are," Ned shot back. "No doubt your lover set them on me. How am I supposed to conduct business with two bozos dogging me all over the world?"

"I'll see what I can do, Ned. But I need money to pay the kidnapper."

"Have the feds front the money."

Closing her eyes, she struggled to keep her tears and her frustrations in check. "I can't do that, Ned. The man who has my son will do God knows what if I involve the authorities."

"From my vantage point, you've already involved the cops. I'd think they'd do anything to help you out, under the circumstances."

"It's more complex than that," Shelby countered. "I've told them all along that you couldn't possibly have anything to do with this."

"I'm sure you told them everything but the truth." A punishing pause followed.

When Shelby refused to rise to the bait, Ned continued. "Then why are they breathing down my neck?" Ned demanded. His voice had risen, and she could almost see his dark eyes bulging from his angry face.

"They think we're enemies."

"Why?"

"Because of what happened before."

"None of that would have happened if you'd kept your nose out of my affairs."

"I've explained all that to you," Shelby groaned. "I never meant to cause you any trouble."

"Well, you did."

"Ned," she said in a pleading tone. "I know you hold me responsible, and maybe I am. But right now I need your help. I need one hundred thousand dollars."

"What makes you think I have that kind of money? My business took a nosedive, thanks to all the negative press."

"Ned..." she began, then stopped, long enough to muster all her courage. "I know all about your secret account in the Caymans. I saw the bank statements."

"I don't know what you're talking about."

"Please, Ned. Don't make this harder than it has to be."

"Me?" he shouted. "I trained you to be a top-notch antiquities dealer. I tried to do right by you, and how did you repay me?"

"I didn't help them!" she countered in a loud whisper. "I backed out and refused to testify about any of the things I suspected you might be doing."

"But not before you put out for that agent."

"Please, Ned," she begged, feeling exhausted. "Believe me, if I had it to do over again, I would never allow myself to be dragged into their investigation."

"But you did. And you damned near cost me my life."

"I'm sorry," she said for the umpteenth time.

"Did you know that?" Ned was plainly seething. "Do you have any idea how close you came to getting me killed?"

"I've said I was sorry, Ned. I have explained to you time and time again that I only answered their questions and worked with Dylan because I believed you were incapable of leading a double life."

"And now?"

"Now what?"

"You left me because you couldn't stand to be around me after Tanner poisoned your mind. But you don't mind taking my money? Is that right?"

"I'll do anything to get my son back."

"How do I know this isn't just another ploy? Just another trick you're helping them execute?"

"I'm not," she told him flatly. "If I didn't tell them what I suspected a year and a half ago, what makes you think I'd do it now?"

"Tanner is back in your life."

"He is not!" Shelby assured him. "He's helping with the investigation."

"That must be cozy."

"Will you help me?" she asked, trying to ignore his cutting sarcasm.

Silence.

"Please."

"I'll have to think about it."

"I don't have the luxury of time. I'm supposed to make the payoff tomorrow night."

Again, silence.

"Ned, I—"

"I'll call you tomorrow morning with my decision."

"Ned—"

She stared at the phone, battling tears. "If he won't help me, what am I going to do?" The heart-wrenching question came out in a hoarse whisper.

"Shelby?"

"Yes?" she responded as she quickly replaced the phone. Shelby wiped the dampness from her cheeks with the back of her hand.

The door creaked open and Dylan slipped into the room. His face contorted into a series of deep lines as his eyes roamed over her face. In an instant he was at her side, the fingers of his hand splayed against her back.

The small gesture was nearly enough to send her into a fit of sobs. Hopelessness manifested itself in the form of a deep ache in her chest. An ache she felt certain would be lessened if only Dylan would hold her.

"What's wrong?" he asked. "Did you find another tape?"

"No," she answered, her voice choked.

"I would do anything to help you," he said, gently pulling her head against his chest. It felt so good, so right. She needed this, needed his strength, if she was going to make it through this without losing her mind. Closing her eyes, Shelby reminded herself that Chad was safe, then surrendered to the promise of comfort she felt in his touch.

Cradling her in one arm, Dylan used his free hand to stroke the hair away from her face. She greedily drank in the scent of his cologne as she cautiously allowed her fingers to rest against his thigh. His jeans were well-worn and smooth, a startling contrast to the very defined muscle she could feel beneath her hand. She remained perfectly still, comforted by his scent, his touch, his nearness. Strange that she could only find such solace in his arms.

"You've got to hang in there," Dylan told her. "We'll find him."

"I hope so," she breathed against his solid form. "I can't close my eyes without seeing his face. Not having Chad is killing me. If it weren't for the tapes, I don't think I could handle it. When I think of what might be—"

"Don't," he murmured. He captured her face in his hands, his callused thumbs wiping away the last vestiges of her tears. His gray-blue eyes met and held hers. His jaw was set, his expression serious. "You can't fall apart, Shelby. You have to stay strong."

"I don't feel very strong," she admitted. "I'm teetering on the edge here. I try not to think about what's happening to him, but—"

"Hush," he said. "He's fine. You have to hold on to that thought. We haven't gotten anything that would indicate Chad has been harmed in any way."

Using his hands, he tilted her head back. His face was a mere fraction of an inch from hers. She could feel the ragged expulsion of his breath. Instinctively her palms flattened against his chest. The thick mat of dark hair served as a cushion for her touch. Still, beneath the softness, she could easily feel the hard outline of muscle.

"I'm here for you," he said in a near whisper.

Her lashes fluttered as his words washed over her upturned face. She'd been expecting it, perhaps even wishing for it. Dylan's lips tentatively brushed hers. So featherlight was the kiss that she wasn't even certain it could qualify as such. His movements were careful, measured. His thumbs stroked the hollows of her cheeks.

Shelby banished all thought from her mind. She wanted this, almost desperately. The sensation of his hands and his lips made her feel alive. The ache in her chest was changing, evolving. The pain and hopelessness were being overtaken by some new emotions. She became acutely aware of every aspect of him. The pressure of his thigh where it touched hers. The sound of his uneven breathing. The magical sensation of his mouth on hers.

When he lifted his head, Shelby grabbed handfuls of his shirt. "Don't," she whispered, urging him back to her.

His resistance was both surprising and short-lived. It was almost totally forgotten when he dipped his head again. His lips did little more than brush against hers. His hands left her face and wound around her small body. Dylan crushed her against him. She could actually feel the pounding of his heart beneath her hands.

What had begun so innocently, quickly turned into something intense and consuming. His tongue moistened her slightly parted lips. The kiss became demanding, and she was a very willing partaker. She managed to work her hands across his chest, until she felt the outline of his erect nipples beneath her palms. He responded by running his hands all over her back and nibbling her lower lip. It was a purely erotic action, one that inspired great need and desire in Shelby.

A small moan escaped her lips as she kneaded the muscles of his chest. He tasted vaguely of coffee, and he continued to work magic with his mouth. Shelby felt the kiss in the pit of her stomach. What had started as a pleasant warmth had grown into a full-fledged heat emanating from her very core, fueled by the sensation of his fingers snaking up her back, entwining in her hair, and guiding her head back at a severe angle. Passion flared as he hungrily devoured first her mouth, then the tender flesh at the base of her throat. His mouth was hot, the stubble of his beard slightly abrasive. And she felt it all. She was aware of everything—the outline of his body, the almost arrogant expectation in his kiss. Dylan was a skilled and talented lover. Shelby was a compliant yet demanding partner.

Jay was knocking on the door.

Reluctantly Dylan lifted his head, his eyes fixed on her mouth. He looked at her with such intensity that Shelby found it almost as carnal as his kisses. She should have uttered some reprimand, or possibly apologized for allowing things to get so heavy. She should have, but she couldn't. She wasn't going to lie to Dylan—not again.

"One second," he called through the closed door. He placed one more kiss against her partially opened mouth. Reluctantly he rose, savoring the taste of her lingering on his lips. She hadn't screamed recriminations—or, worse yet, voiced regrets.

Ignoring Jay's questioning once-over, Dylan moved to allow his boss into the room. He turned to find Shelby seated on the bed, looking right at him.

Her eyes were still hooded by her heavy lids. Her lips were slightly red from the imprint of his kiss. He looked again for some negative sign. There was none. In fact, he detected just the trace of a smile at the corners of her mouth.

"I thought we should start by watching this," Jay was saying.

"I suppose it's too much to hope that the lab guys got anything off the cassette?" Dylan asked.

"No such luck," Jay answered.

"Is Chad on the tape?" Shelby asked as Jay bent forward to insert the tape.

"Yep. And he looks like he's in great shape."

Dylan watched as the light in her eyes flickered, then was extinguished, like the flame from a faltering candle. Her small body stiffened as she scooted to the edge of the bed.

Dylan wanted desperately to go to her, to take her back into his arms. To protect her from Nichols and his cohorts.

"We've drawn a blank on the location," Jay admitted as he pressed the play button. "We know it's somewhere on one of the islands."

"The barrier islands?" Shelby's voice was tight and even when she formed the question.

"Looks that way. At least that's what I got from the lab boys. Something about the vegetation in the shot."

The blue screen gave way to the image of the smiling baby, which Dylan would have recognized anywhere. Chad was in the same stroller they'd seen in the earlier tape.

He heard Shelby's sharp intake of breath when the camera zoomed in on the child. The baby was pounding a set of keys against the stroller. In the background, he could make out some sort of construction site. Stacks of lumber surrounded elaborate scaffolding.

The baby began to babble—a stream of nonsensical consonants punctuated with a continual stream of drool. The camera pulled back until the frame included the right foot of a person. More specifically, a woman.

"Are we assuming it's the same person?" Dylan asked.

"No reason not to," Jay answered.

There was the obligatory placement of the newspaper in the frame with the baby. This time the woman balanced the paper against the baby's feet. The camera caught the date, and then the tape ended.

"Not much help," Jay admitted apologetically.

"Yes, it is," Shelby said. "I know exactly where that was taken."

Chapter Fifteen

"You know where it is?" Dylan asked, excitedly grabbing her shoulders.

"It's the Vanderhorst mansion on Kiawah Island."

"Kiawah?" Jay asked.

Dylan smiled down at her, his eyes hopeful. Shelby noted that the senior agent's expression was guarded. She suspected his hesitation was a direct result of the lack of success they'd had thus far. Secretly she thought it was kind of Jay to be so concerned. Perhaps he, too, had recognized the aging building and had said nothing to spare her yet another heartbreak. Or maybe they'd just taped her call to Ned.

"I'll head out there," Dylan announced.

"Why don't you go with him, Shelby?" Jay suggested.

Dylan turned away from her, but not before she saw a frown overtake his chiseled lips.

"I don't think that's necessary," she heard Dylan tell Jay.

Jay simply shrugged. "I do."

"Jay," Dylan began, his hands balled into loose fists at his sides, "there's no point in sending her on what could turn out to be another wild-goose chase."

Shelby felt the first twinges of annoyance. She didn't like being discussed as if she were invisible. "I'd like to go."

Dylan spun around, and his eyes bored into hers. "Do you really think you can handle another disappointment?"

"What makes you so sure this will be a disappointment?"

"I'm not saying it will be. Not definitely," he said. Falling down on one knee, he knelt in front of her, gathering her small hands in his much larger ones. "I know how all this is affecting you."

She cut in. "Do you? I don't think you can even imagine the anguish I feel. Chad is my whole world."

"I understand that," Dylan said soothingly. "That's why I'm not so sure it's a good idea for you to come along. Why not let me check it out first?"

"Because he's my son. Because I want to be there when he's found—to reassure him. But mostly because I can't stand sitting around here, just waiting."

Long after Dylan and Jay had left her alone, Shelby began to reassess her motivations. She believed the argument she had given Dylan, but she was beginning to acknowledge that there might be more to it. "I'm losing my mind," she grumbled as she reached over and allowed her hand to slap the pillow next to her. Just being with Dylan was comforting. When he held her, she actually believed that everything would be all right. That Chad would be returned safe and sound.

The room still cradled the faint scent of Dylan's cologne. She could close her eyes and his image was there, gorgeous and dangerous. "I should be doing everything possible to shut him out of my life," she murmured, her whispered voice full of self-loathing.

It was true. As easy as it was to lean on him now, how easy would it be to say goodbye—again? Turning on her side, Shelby hugged the pillow to her breast and tried to formulate a plausible plan. Nothing seemed to work. Not one of the scenarios she considered was pleasant. Her mind kept going backward in time. Replaying that ugly scene when she'd told him it was over. The image of his seething face was one she would carry for all time. It had been a year and a half, and still she could vividly see the fury behind the stiff set of his jaw. She could still feel the pressure on her arms from where he'd bruisingly grabbed her and kissed her farewell in that hurtful, derisive fashion. The thought of having to experience all that again sent her heart plummeting in her feet. But she had no choice.

"WHAT'S THE PLAN?" she asked as Dylan threw the Blazer in gear.

He laughed softly and said, "We don't have one. We're checking out the possibilities, not conducting a raid."

"I know that," she said, defensively. "I was just asking."

They drove several miles in silence. Shelby was aware of everything. The way his large body filled the small confines of the passenger compartment; the way his thumb kept time with the soft rock tune on the radio; the way the heavy air spilling through the partially open window lifted his black hair off his collar. She wiggled against the soft upholstery, trying to figure out just what had gotten into her.

The low country varied little, mile after mile. Tall sea grasses lined marshy swamps as the various rivers surrounding Charleston converged on the Atlantic. Kiawah Island, she knew from her days selling pricey antiquities, was a posh resort south of the city. The barrier island was essentially divided in half. One portion of the land was devoted to the tourist trade—shops, restaurants, golf courses and tennis courts. The remainder of the island sported some of the largest, most expensive and elegant private properties in the area. Her first trip to Kiawah had been something of a shock. What she originally mistook for a conference center had turned out to be an individual home, all 7,500 square feet of it—facing the gentle surf of the Atlantic.

"Why are we going to the inn?" Shelby asked. "The Vanderhorst mansion is in the property owners' section."

"I know that," Dylan answered as he pulled into a parking spot.

"But you told Jay you were going to touch base with island security."

Dylan turned and lifted his mirrored glasses from his eyes. "I'm taking a different approach."

"Why?"

Clipping the glasses to the front of his polo shirt, Dylan leaned closer. "I'm taking a new tack."

"Which is?"

"Spontaneous investigation." Reaching out with one square-tipped finger, he lightly tapped the end of her nose. "It's a trick I learned in agent school."

He moved from the car in fluid movements. Shelby followed closely on his heels, her eyes fixed on the broad expanse of his shoulders. She made the mistake of lowering her eyes. His jeans hugged his slender hips, outlining his masculine curves. She swallowed, hard.

Reaching back, Dylan clasped her hand in his. His skin was warm, his grip firm. In an attempt to keep her mind focused, Shelby began to catalog the various flowers lining the walkway. A small twinge of emotion tugged at her heart. Chad was just developing a fascination with flowers.

The entrance to the Kiawah Inn was a skeleton of weathered wood framing, decorated with massive hanging baskets of spring flowers. The sweet floral fragrance was carried on the warm ocean breezes wafting through the walkway.

Dylan eased her close to the banister to allow a couple to pass. The pair walked with that bouncy, happy step often reserved for vacationers. Shelby envied them.

As they passed the lobby, the air suddenly filled with the inviting smells coming off the poolside grill. The distant hum of a lawn mower was interrupted by an occasional squeal of pure delight coming from the beach.

"We'll start here," Dylan announced when they came upon a bicycle-rental stand at the end of the ribbon of fine-grained sand.

"Start what?"

"I thought we might want to go in the back door."

Dylan reached into the front pocket of his jeans and peeled several bills off to give to the young attendant. They were directed to a pair of neon-orange bikes at the end of the rack.

"I'm assuming you can ride a bike?"

"I could when I was seven," she muttered under her breath. She looked from the bike to her clothes and frowned. She had abandoned her jeans in favor of a gauzy sundress. The uneven handkerchief hem threatened to be a problem.

"Here," Dylan said, reaching for the bottom of the dress.

"What on earth?" she cried as he folded the fabric and tucked the ends into the belt at her waist. His fingers worked deftly, arranging the garment until it was immodestly short, resting very near the top of her thighs. Shelby remained perfectly still. It was her only choice, since she was firm in her resolve not to react to the feel of his hands brushing the skin of her bared legs.

His head came up, and he wore a decidedly satisfied smile. "That should keep it out of your way."

"And I'll be giving free shots to everyone I pass." Shelby tugged and wriggled until the hemline dropped a couple of inches.

"Ready?" he asked.

"Yes," she answered as she threw one leg over the bike. "Would you mind telling me what I'm ready for?"

"A leisurely ride along the beach."

"Dylan!" she breathed. "We're supposed to be looking for my son. I don't think this is a particularly good time for one of your silly little—"

His hard stare stilled the words in her throat. She sensed his anger long before he lifted his glasses and she saw the harsh glint in his eyes.

"This isn't a silly anything." He forced the words out between nearly gritted teeth. "If you don't like the way I'm handling this, feel free to go on home. I didn't ask you to come along in the first place."

She flinched at the unexpected venom. Not knowing the cause of his uncharacteristic attack, she simply stared at him through wide, confused eyes.

"I'm sorry," he said, after several deep breaths. "All I can say is that I'm on edge about all of this."

"You think something's gone wrong?" she asked, grabbing his forearm.

"No, no. Nothing like that. I'm just bugged."

"By what?" she queried, studying the deep, telling lines around his eyes.

"All of this," he answered disgustedly.

"*Please,* be more specific."

Dylan took his foot off the pedal and stood straddling the bike. Placing his glasses on the bridge of his slightly crooked nose, he raked his hand through his windblown hair. "Something just isn't right," he said.

"Dylan?"

"Like I said before. this guy always seems to be a half step ahead of us." He slapped the handlebars in apparent frustration. "It's like Nichols has a pipeline into my head."

"Dylan," she began, in a purposefully soft voice, "I know you want to believe it's Ned. But he's not even in the country. And he has no reason to want to hurt my baby."

"His baby, too," Dylan said gruffly.

"And what did you mean about your head?"

His shoulders rose and fell in a quick shrug. "I'm starting to feel manipulated."

God! she thought as panic swelled in her chest. *He's finally put it all together!*

"I never meant for you to—"

"Not by you." He patted the back of her hand, where it rested against his arm. "I know you haven't exactly welcomed me on this investigation. It's this perp. I feel like he's pulling my strings."

"Is the sun getting to you?" she asked.

"I'm serious," he insisted, the corners of his mouth curving downward to form the beginnings of a frown. "This is the weirdest case I've every encountered. There's something here I'm missing."

"I think you're allowing your frustrations to cloud your perspective," Shelby said. *Was it possible? Could he somehow sense his close connection to the baby? How long would it be before he uncovered her deceptions?*

"It's more than that," he insisted with a shake of his head. "First the medallion, then a tape shows up at my apartment. Let's not forget the video left in the car yesterday. I mean—'' he paused and ran his fingers pensively across the faint stubble on his chin ''—how in the hell did this guy know we'd be downtown? Let alone that he'd have enough time to slip into your car without leaving so much as a loose fiber behind?''

Shelby's relief regarding the issue of her son's parentage was short-lived. Instantly her mind replayed the phone call she'd gotten in the bath shop. He must have followed them into Charleston. After renewing the ransom demand, the kidnapper must have seen them go down Market Street. But she couldn't say anything to Dylan, for to do so would only jeopardize her last hope of remaining in the kidnapper's good graces. She understood how he could have delivered the tape to her parked car in the city. Dylan's medallion, and the other things, weren't so easily explained.

''Shelby?''

She came back to the present with a jolt.

''I'm sorry,'' he said.

''About what?''

''Obviously, I upset you.''

''I'm fine,'' she lied. ''Where to?''

''We'll ride down the beach and then cut over to the mansion.''

''Forgive me,'' she said as she balanced herself on the slow-moving bicycle, ''but why can't we just drive up and check it out?''

''You saw all the construction debris?'' She nodded. ''I think we might have more success if we used the subtle approach.''

''The subtle approach to what?''

"Just trust me," he said as his powerful thighs pumped effortlessly carrying him over the packed sand. "And no matter what happens, follow my lead."

The beach was nearly deserted. Wispy white clouds floated overhead as they rode side by side at the edge of the rolling surf. The sand was flat near the water, and the cool spray coming off the surf kept her from feeling the exertion of keeping up with his pace.

"Doing okay?" he said above the call of a gull.

"For now," she told him. "My legs will probably be screaming at me later."

"What? You don't spend hours in some gym, praying to the god of fitness?"

She laughed easily. "I think the last time I broke a sweat was when Chad was born."

Steering with one hand, Dylan turned and stole a quick glance in her direction. "Was it tough?"

"What?"

"Having him? My sister told me it was like having her lower lip pulled over her skull."

"Just about," Shelby said through her laughter. "I didn't know you had a sister."

"Three."

"Three sisters?"

"And two brothers."

Shelby gaped at him. "Six children? Your mother deserves a medal."

"No argument from me," he said as he slowed his bike. "We didn't give her a moment of peace. Let's take a break."

Following his lead, Shelby brought her bike to a stop, pulled the kickstand, and parked it in the sand next to his. Her legs didn't adjust immediately to the flat ground.

Shading her eyes with her hand, she looked back at the inn. "I didn't realize," she gushed, feeling suddenly tired.

"We've come about five miles. I thought you might need a breather."

"I'll probably need physical therapy," she stated as she fell into the sand next to him.

Dylan leaned back, resting his weight on his bent forearms. With his legs crossed at the ankles, he appeared totally relaxed.

"Want me to tell you about my family?" he asked.

"Why?"

He didn't look at her, and she couldn't see anything but her own reflection in those damned glasses.

"You said that we didn't know anything about each other. I figured my family might be a good place to start." He interpreted her silence as acquiescence. "I grew up in a small town in New York—in the Catskills."

"Did you have the largest family in town?"

"Hardly." She could hear the smile in his voice. "Loganville is a staunchly Catholic town. Everyone was fruitful and multiplied."

"Did you have block parties and forts and a carnival that came to town every summer?"

"You bet," he said as his finger began to trace a geometric pattern in the small strip of sand separating them. "We had PTA and youth groups, bake sales and Little League."

"Sounds like a nice place."

"It is."

"Do you ever go back?" she asked.

"Every chance I get. Of course, Thanksgiving is mandatory. My mother has promised to put a curse on any of her children who fail to show up for her favorite holiday."

"Thanksgiving? Why then?"

"I think it has something to do with control. Christmas and Easter were really hard on my folks. Since both sets of grandparents also lived in Loganville, the big holidays were nothing but marathons that began with early mass and ended with one of us kids barfing from eating too many sweets. Thanksgiving was her day."

"I can't imagine getting six kids organized to do anything. I often have trouble managing Chad, and he's a pretty adaptable little guy."

"I can imagine." His expression grew solemn before he asked, "Why did you do it, Shelby? I mean, you didn't have to go through with it."

"I already told you. Chad was a surprise, but I never even once considered terminating my pregnancy."

"What do you plan to tell him?"

"About what?"

"You know." Dylan paused and sucked in a great lungful of the fresh sea air. "About his father."

"I'll explain to him that I had the right child with the wrong man."

"Think he'll buy it?"

Shelby felt herself stiffen under his direct scrutiny. "I don't know. I guess I'll cross that bridge when I get there." Sitting up, she hugged her legs with her arms. "Tell me more about your family."

"Typical big family."

"Meaning?"

"We fought constantly amongst ourselves, but heaven help the outsider that dared lay a finger on any of us. Especially the girls."

"Why the girls?"

"You kidding?" he asked as he joined her by drawing his long legs to his chest. "Would you have wanted three older brothers screening your dates?"

"Probably," she admitted in a soft voice.

"No brothers?"

She shook her head.

"Sisters?"

"Nope."

"Your folks only wanted one child?"

"No, but my father never resented me for it." She gathered her hair at the nape of her neck to prevent it blowing on her face.

"Come again?" Dylan said.

"Chadwick Hunnicutt married my mother when I was two. He adopted me shortly after they got married."

"What about your real father?"

"He was my real father," Shelby told him stiffly.

"I didn't say that right," Dylan said apologetically. "I just meant, do you have any contact with your birth father?"

Shelby swallowed. How had she allowed the conversation to turn to this most unpleasant subject—and with him, of all people? "Not really. I don't really know him."

"Do you speak?"

"Occasionally," she said carefully. "It's very complicated, and I don't really like discussing it."

"How does he feel about Chad?"

"He's about as good at being a grandfather as he was at being a father."

"I can't imagine not having my family," Dylan said, draping his arm lazily over her shoulder. "Thanks to them, I have a whole bunch of great memories."

"Such as?" she asked, hoping a turn in the direction of the conversation might help her think of something other than the feel of his skin touching hers.

"There was the time we wrecked the station wagon."

"That's a great memory?" she asked.

"We rolled the family station wagon coming down one of the mountains. No one was hurt. We rolled it back on its wheels, and then swore to my pop that we didn't have a clue how the car got all banged up."

"Did he buy it?"

"Hell, no!" he recalled, with genuine fondness. "It took us the better part of two years to pay for the damage out of our allowances."

"What does your father do?"

"He's a butcher."

"Then what made you become a cop?"

"I guess it was all those nights I dusted my little sisters for prints when they came home from their dates."

"Cute," Shelby said, swatting him.

"I'm not kidding. My sisters are gorgeous."

"So you thought they were easy?"

"No, but I knew how persuasive young men could be after a few hours in the back of a Chevy."

"From personal experience?"

"I preferred to think of it as research," he said with a devilish grin. "My contribution to the family."

"What a guy," she said under her breath.

"I am a nice guy, Shelby. You just didn't stick around long enough to find out."

"Dylan," she groaned, "let's not beat this dead horse, okay?"

"For now," he said as he hoisted his large frame off the cool sand.

Extending his hand, he helped her to feet. He held her hand a fraction longer than necessary. Shelby was still struggling with her conscience. For the first time, she questioned her decision, thanks in large part to the things he'd said. *Why didn't he tell me of his family before? If he had, would I still have walked away?*

True to his prediction, they pedaled for another five or so miles before they came upon a smooth wooden board-walk that traversed the protected dunes. After they abandoned the bikes, near the path, Dylan took her hand as he got his bearings. He liked the feel of her hand in his. Her skin was so perfectly soft, her hand so small and fragile. Even her feet were tiny, he noted as they walked side by side. The toenails peeking out of her leather sandals were painted pale pink, yet another tribute to the incredible femininity that had attracted him to Shelby that first night.

Only this was harder. He felt a weighty responsibility to find her son. If he didn't—or, God forbid, if it ended badly—he didn't think she would survive.

"What *exactly* are we doing?"

"We're going to the construction site," he said as they passed yet another palatial home.

"I still don't see why we didn't just drive on up and ask for their help."

"You will," he said, then mentally added, *I hope.*

The mansion was off what was considered the main road in the residential section of the island. Kiawah was a far cry from his humble beginnings. These were stately, individually designed buildings with landscaped lawns and perfectly pruned live oaks. He guessed even the Spanish moss needed permission to hang from the trees. The royal palms and evergreens on the road's median strip were identical heights, and evenly spaced. Even the wildflowers had an air of decorum.

Crossing the perfectly surfaced road, they came upon a dirt road covered in a thin layer of pine straw. The relatively undisturbed forest was thick with the smell of soldered metal and sawdust. Dylan felt at home with the scent of manual labor. It eased the knot of tension between his shoulder blades.

Sidestepping a makeshift barricade, he pulled Shelby behind him, down what had obviously once been a driveway. It was guarded on either side by overgrown oak trees. Portions of the brick-and-wood home were visible about fifty yards ahead of them. Workmen buzzed from place to place as they tended to the various responsibilities of renovating the dilapidated landmark.

"Tory would be like a kid in a candy shop here," she said.

"Why?"

"This place dates back to before the Civil War. It's the kind of preservation and restoration project she's been studying for years. Since these kinds of jobs are few and far between, she's after Rose and I to let her excavate and renovate the outbuildings at the Tattoo."

"She's definitely still in school, then?"

"Of course," she answered. "Rose and I try to help her whenever we can."

"Hey, you! Can't you read?"

The man coming toward them wore a hard hat and a frown. Dylan stopped short, and gave Shelby's hand a squeeze. "Go along with whatever I say."

"What do you mean?"

"This area ain't safe," the worker announced as he tugged up the tool belt surrounding his thick waist. "It ain't open to tourists."

Dylan extended his hand and said, "I appreciate that, Mr.... er..."

"Bo Halloday."

"Mr. Halloday," Dylan continued, "we don't want to disturb your work. My wife and I were just curious about something, and hoping you, or one of your men, might be able to help us."

Wife? she gulped.

"Help you what?" The man eyed him seriously. His weathered, leathery skin bunched at the corners of his mistrustful eyes.

"You see," he began, slipping his free hand into his breast pocket. "We think our nanny has been bringing Chad over here. We know how dangerous this area is, and we'll want to discourage her from placing him in any danger."

Nanny?

Halloday gripped the photo between dirty, honest fingers. "Cute kid."

"Have you seen him in his stroller? Perhaps you had to run them off in the past couple of days?"

Halloday yelled over his shoulder. A young man, lanky and shirtless, sprinted over to them. His T-shirt, which had been wrapped around his head, was grimy and damp. The stench of sweat was almost overwhelming.

"Tommy Ray? Is this the kid what was here with that lady yesterday?"

The boy took the picture and then bobbed his head. "I believe so," he said. "Nice boy. The man and the lady was real nice, too. Even when I had to tell them to move on."

"Man?" Dylan heard Shelby gasp.

"A tall guy, wearing a hat and sunglasses."

"What about the woman?" Dylan asked.

"Nice smile," the two men said in unison. "And she sure did dote on that baby," added Tommy.

Dylan gave Shelby's hand another squeeze, surprised at the amount of relief he felt on hearing that Chad was being well cared for. "Did you see them leave?"

"Watched until they got into their car."

"What kind of car?"

"American," the younger man said. "I'm pretty sure it was a black Taurus."

Dylan thanked them before tugging Shelby back in the direction of the bikes.

"Where are we going now?" she asked. "Do you think we'll be able to find them by just knowing the kind of car? I hope he was right. I hope this woman is taking decent care of him. I hate to think of my baby in the arms—"

He pulled her against him, cradling her excitement-flushed face in his hands. "Calm down," he told her. "I don't know if we'll be able to find them, but we've got a couple of leads. I think you ought to go back to town while I see if I can't get something more substantial."

"No," she said as her hands came up to close over his. "I don't want to go home, Dylan. I can't stand just sitting around and waiting. I need to keep busy."

He closed his eyes to wrestle with his misgivings. An intelligent man would send her packing. A smart agent would recognize the potential danger of having a private citizen involved in his investigation.

"I don't want you to go, either."

Chapter Sixteen

"Let's head back to the inn," Dylan suggested as they walked hand in hand toward the beach.

"What was all that stuff about a wife and nanny?" she asked.

She felt him shrug his shoulders. "Just playing it safe."

"Is this the same man who had nothing nice to say about the institution of marriage?"

"When did I ever comment on marriage?" he asked, stopping and tugging on her hand until she peered up into her own reflection in his glasses.

"You told me you'd been engaged. I believe your exact words were 'one arrest, no conviction.'"

His mouth curved into a sheepish half smile. "It was just an analogy, Shelby."

"But you made your point," she told him in a soft voice, her eyes dropping to the open V of his shirt. Dark curls peeked from the edges, set against tanned skin.

"I wasn't trying to make a point."

She could hear the frown in his voice, and his grip on her hand tightened fractionally. Tension enveloped her, and she refused to look up.

"If I remember correctly," he began, his hand stroking the faint stubble on his chin, "we'd been out maybe three or four times when I made that crack."

"It's not important," she insisted, forcing cheer into her tone. Turning, she pulled her hand free of his and began to walk. "I don't know how we got on this inane subject, anyway."

"I believe in marriage," Dylan said, very close to her ear. "When I made that comment, I was just trying to be cute."

"Fine," she said on a breath. "Let's drop it."

"Does this have anything to do with why you dumped me?"

"Dylan," she groaned. "I don't want to talk about it. It's ancient history."

"I suppose," he said as his hand snaked back to hers.

The sound of the surf acted as a tonic to her frazzled nerves. Why, she wondered, did walking with him, holding his hand, feel so right?

Her legs screamed in silent protest when she mounted the bike. Her spirits began to plummet. "What are we going to do now?" she asked as she pulled her bike next to his.

Dylan's legs were working at less than half the rate of her own. Leaning back on the seat, he guided his bike with only one hand through the damp sand at the water's edge.

"I'm thinking on it."

"Shouldn't we be scouring the island for a black Taurus?"

"Maybe."

"Well, I don't think we'll get much accomplished riding down the beach."

"Maybe."

Reaching out, Shelby swatted his sleeve before resuming her death grip on the handlebars. "Are you being intentionally obtuse?"

His chuckle was deep and throaty. The sound stroked her from the top of her head down to her toes.

"Obtuse?" he repeated. "Hardly. I'm simply devising a plan. The federal government prefers it that way. It's one of the first things they teach you in agent school."

"I'm just impatient, Dylan. I want my son back."

"I know you do," he said, touching the skin on her arm, just above the elbow. "I'll find him."

The sincerity behind his words threatening to inspire tears, Shelby swallowed and lowered her eyes.

"Watch out!" Dylan yelled.

She looked up in time to see the blurred colors of a kite as it wrapped around her face. The next several seconds involved large quantities of sand and water, and a hard collision with Dylan's even harder body. They were a tangled mass of legs, spokes and wet paper.

She came up coughing, trying to expel some of the salty water from her lungs.

"You wrecked it!"

Blinking against the stinging water, Shelby braced herself upright as waves washed over her sodden form. The face of a very angry young boy came in to focus. "Wh-what?"

"You wrecked my kite," he yelled.

Before she could respond to the charge, Dylan reached around her waist and hoisted her from the surf. Her dress hung heavily from her shoulders, and she could feel her hair plastered to her cheeks.

"You okay?" Dylan asked.

"No," she groaned as she pulled the soaked fabric away from her legs. "I'm drenched and I have sand in my mouth."

"And you wrecked my kite."

"Sorry about that, pal," Dylan told the child.

Just then, a harried-looking woman with several ounces of white sunscreen lathered on her nose ran over to them.

"I'm so sorry," she began, her hand gripping the child's upper arm. "Are you two all right?"

Dylan answered for them both. "No harm done."

"I told you to keep the kite up near the dunes," the mother said to her son.

"It's okay," Dylan insisted.

The woman offered a weak, apologetic smile as she tugged the little boy up the beach.

"This is awful," Shelby groaned. But as she looked up through her wet, clumped lashes, her annoyance abruptly melted.

"What?" Dylan asked.

Getting up on tiptoe, she extracted the bulbous strand of seaweed from the earpiece of his sunglasses with two fingers. She could feel the warmth emanating from his large body.

His eyes met and held hers. "Thanks."

The space between them filled with an electric current of awareness. His wet shirt clung to the etched definition of muscle, drawing her eyes like a magnet, and the tumble had caused it to work free of his jeans, exposing several inches of his firm, taut skin.

"Now what?" she asked, in a rather high-pitched voice.

"I think a pit stop is in order," he told her with a grin. "We'll see what we can do back at the inn."

He was smiling as he stood at the registration desk, his charge card in his hand. Shelby lingered near the doorway, half hidden by a large potted plant. After accepting a key from the clerk, he collected Shelby and led her to the elevator. They got more than just a few looks from passing vacationers.

"What good will a shower do?" she asked as he slipped the key into the lock. "I'll never get the sand out of my clothes."

"I'll handle it," Dylan insisted as he shoved open the door and stood aside. When she passed beneath his outstretched hand, he caught the faint scent of the ocean in her hair. He took a deep breath and reminded himself that he was here to do a job.

He left her and went across to the straw market. Discovering a trendy clothing shop, he selected some items for them and prayed his credit card could withstand the outrageous total. With the package tucked neatly beneath his arm, he headed back toward the inn. He didn't go directly to the room. Instead, he found the pay phone, dug into the soggy contents of his pocket and slipped a coin into the slot.

"Williams."

"Jay. Dylan," he began, cradling the phone between his shoulder and ear.

"Find anything?"

"Maybe. We might have a lead on the car."

"Really?"

"Didn't one of the neighbors say he'd seen a black car on the night Chad was taken?"

There was a brief pause, and Dylan could hear the sounds of papers shuffling before Jay said, "Yep. But he wasn't able to ID the make or model."

Dylan recounted their trip to the mansion, omitting the mishap at the end. "We're at the Kiawah Inn," he said, adding the room number.

"You two are together?"

Dylan felt his spine stiffen at the censure he heard in his boss's tone. "Just a home base while we look for the car."

"Why don't I send a car for Shelby? She's—"

"She won't budge," Dylan said, cutting in. "As long as there's a snowball's chance that we might find her son, she won't go anywhere."

"Are you sure it's Shelby and not you?"

Dylan drew his brows together and wondered why that remark should inspire such anger in him. "Meaning?"

"Look, Dylan," Jay began, "I know you had a thing for her last—"

"It's history," he said sternly.

"Yours or hers?"

An answer sprang to his lips—*hers*. But he kept it to himself. A silence ensued, a rather awkward one.

Jay relented. "I'll contact the management for the island and see if I can get any information on the car. I'll call you if I can find any residents who drive a black Taurus."

"Thanks, Jay."

"Speaking of calls—there have been three hang-ups here at her place. It's probably the kidnapper."

"Probably," Dylan agreed, a strange feeling settling in his gut. Something disturbing, yet he was unable to give it a name or even guess at its origins. "He's slipping."

"How so?" Jay countered.

"He's usually pretty adept at making contact with Shelby, no matter where she is."

"You're right about that," Jay lamented. "It's like this guy has radar where she's concerned."

Anger surged through Dylan. He'd find this guy, and when he did, he'd make sure he paid. He suggested as much to Jay.

"Careful, Tanner," Jay cautioned. "I wouldn't want to see you lose your objectivity."

I lost it a year and a half ago, he thought. "I'm objective enough. I'll keep you posted."

When he returned to the room, he heard the unmistakable sound of the shower running. Depositing the package on the end of the king-size bed that dominated the room, Dylan battled to keep his thoughts on track. Unfortunately, his mind seemed intent on traveling beyond the closed door. The image of Shelby standing beneath the spray of water inspired any number of fantasies.

"Stupid," he mumbled as he separated the clothing into two piles. Letting out a breath, he frowned, remembering their brief conversation on the beach. When he told her about his short engagement, he hadn't meant her to take it as an indictment of marriage. He could only wonder how many other comments he'd made that she might have misconstrued. Could their breakup have been avoided by a simple conversation? That possibility darkened his mood.

"Why the scowl?"

His head whipped around at the sound of her voice. She gripped the top edges of the terry-cloth towel in white-knuckled fingers. Her dark hair was combed back, and her oval face held the rosy blush of the sun and wind. The scent of flowers filled the room, a fresh, clean scent.

"Scowl?" he repeated, forcing a smile to his lips. "I guess I was just deep in thought."

He watched as her features grew wide, frightened. "There haven't been any new developments, have there?"

He shook his head. The action caused a small cascade of sand to flutter to the floor. "Nothing new."

She visibly relaxed, her bowlike mouth forming a relieved smile. "Thank goodness."

He allowed his eyes to fall to the hem of the towel, where it grazed her legs at midthigh. She had great legs, firm but not muscular, perfectly delicate.

"Dylan?"

"Huh?" he managed over the lump in his throat.

"Clothes?"

"Right," he said as he reached behind him and grabbed one of the stacks. He thrust them in her direction, his eyes fixed on her tenuous hold on the towel.

"Thanks," she mumbled as she grabbed the items and held them against her. She slipped back behind the door, leaving him alone with his vivid imagination.

He didn't dare sit—not when he had a good portion of the beach in his clothes. It was just as well. The act of pacing allowed him a physical action to counter his emotional purgatory. Opening the sliding glass door, Dylan stepped onto the room's small balcony. His hands wrapped around the cool metal railing as he sucked in deep breaths and took in the panoramic view of the ocean. The sun was to his back, casting a long orange shadow on the high tide. He needed to get a grip, and fast. He just couldn't seem to get past this. He had been so sure that he was over Shelby, that she was just a painful memory.

"It's all yours."

He turned and felt his breath catch in his throat. Shelby looked like an angel, a vision in white. The dress he'd selected for her was simple. The clerk had called it a slip dress and insisted that it was appropriate. Now he knew why. Thin straps held the equally thin material against her body, leaving very little to his already overworked imagination. The stark contrast of the white silk against her darkly exotic coloring caused a predictable reaction in his body. Dylan very nearly ran into the bathroom, chased by his guilty conscience.

He stood under a punishing spray of cold water, berating himself for allowing his primal thoughts to get the better of him. He decided to concentrate on the case. He was still bugged by the inconsistencies. The idea that he was missing something crucial gnawed at him almost as much as the memory of Shelby in that dress.

Clearing a circle in the condensation on the mirror, Dylan smiled at the assortment of toiletries in a basket on the vanity. Of course, for what this place charged for a room, he felt it was almost fitting that the inn provided all the comforts of home. After shaving, he ran a comb through his hair and pulled on the khaki shorts he'd bought and shrugged into the shirt. Spotting a plastic laundry bag in the corner, he added his sandy offerings and pulled the drawstring.

"I feel much better," he announced as he strode from the bathroom.

She was on the balcony, her ebony hair floating off her shoulders in the breeze. She smiled when she spotted him. He found the action disconcerting.

"You look better," she teased.

"I thought women liked gritty, unkempt men."

"This woman doesn't."

He moved closer, until mere inches separated them. She rose slowly, her head tilted up toward him. Her eyes were wide, and so very blue.

"Now what?" she asked softly.

"Jay's checking on the car. He'll call when he has something. And he said they still haven't been able to trace the insignia on the ring."

Her lashes fluttered against her cheeks before she peered up at him. "That wasn't what I was talking about."

Dylan held his breath and went still.

"I . . ." she began softly. Her small hands moved to his chest, the palms flattening against him.

His body shivered involuntarily at her touch. He was afraid to move, afraid he might somehow break the spell.

"Tell me what you want, Shelby."

He saw the raw emotions in her eyes, everything from fear to desire. He prayed desire would win out.

"You," she said on a whisper. "I want you, Dylan. I know this is crazy, but I need to be close to you. I'm not quite as scared when you hold me."

He framed her face with his large, warm hands. He felt her shiver as the tips of his thumbs grazed her lips.

He kissed the corners of her mouth as his hands glided down her spine to her hips. When her arms twined around his neck, he lifted his head and looked into her eyes.

"Are you sure?" he asked.

"Very."

Urgency surged through him, setting fire to his blood. Scooping her up in his arms, he pulled her against his chest and carried her to the bed. He set her down amid the assortment of pillows. He settled next to her, arranging her hair to grant him access to the sweet skin of her throat. He kissed, nibbled and tasted. She responded by kneading the muscles at his shoulders and twisting her small body against his. Her actions turned his stomach to liquid and caused an unrelenting ache in his lower body.

Fanning his fingers against her flat stomach, he felt the effect his kisses were having. His mouth hungrily found hers. She made a small sound against his lips when his hand moved higher, until his knuckles brushed against the underside of her breast. His mouth moved lower, until he tasted the skin at her throat. Shelby caught his head between her hands and her fingers through his hair. He kissed the hollow, then stroked every inch of her collarbone with his mouth. Catching one strap between his teeth, Dylan smoothed it off her shoulder.

He heard her suck in her breath when his hand moved up to close possessively over her breast. He could feel her taut nipple straining against his palm. He squeezed gently.

Lifting his head, he felt satisfaction spill through his system when he saw the flush of desire on her cheeks. He captured her lower lip with his mouth, tugging gently as his hand slipped beneath the silky fabric. Cupping her breast in his hand, he kissed her hard as his thumb teased her nipple. Her response became more urgent as she pressed against him.

Her hands tore at his shirt, pushing the fabric down to trap his arms. Dylan lifted away from her long enough to shed the shirt and look and admire his prize. The dress had worked its way to her waist, and he caressed her with his eyes. It was a heady experience, looking down at her. Her erratic breathing and desire-glazed eyes were almost enough to send him over the edge.

Caging her with his arms, Dylan dipped his head and placed a hard kiss against her open mouth. His tongue teased hers, then moved lower.

She moaned in earnest when his mouth closed over one breast. He kissed the soft valley between her breasts, then moved his attentions to the other.

"Dylan..." She said his name on a rush of breath. "Dylan, please..."

He lifted his head, and she arched against him, communicating her need. Her fingers moved through the hair on his chest until she discovered his nipples. Lifting her head from the pillow, Shelby kissed him as he had kissed her. He watched her as her hands eagerly explored the contours of his body. They slipped around him, then moved lower. Shelby held his hips firmly against hers. Now it was his turn to moan.

Catching her chin with his finger, Dylan tilted her face toward his and kissed her passionately as he used his knee to spread her legs. He settled against her, feeling smugly male when she reacted to the unmistakable sign of his desire.

He wanted this moment to last forever. He felt her need, and it rivaled his own. Her hands molded to his hips, as she matched his rhythm. Slowly he slid his hands down her side, stopping briefly to explore the soft weight of her breasts.

"Dylan," she said against his mouth.

He brushed a kiss across her forehead. "Yes?"

Her hands began a frantic search for his zipper. Dylan accommodated her by rolling off to one side. He captured one pert nipple in his mouth as she fumbled with the snap. The rasp of metal on metal was followed by the relief of the intense pressure of confinement. When her fingertip slipped beneath the waistband of his shorts, Dylan tensed and silently begged for control. If she touched him, he knew, it would be over too soon.

Capturing her wrist, he brought her hand to his mouth and placed several kisses against her palm. Their eyes met in a long, silent dialogue of need. He placed her hand against his chest. She immediately began an exploration of the tense muscles at his neck. Balancing on his forearms, Dylan's eyes remained fixed on her as he slowly ground himself against her, reveling in the heat emanating from her body. She arched against him, her mouth seeking his. Dylan countered her actions, but maintained the slow gyration of his hips.

Her movements became more insistent. He felt her feet wrap around his ankles, joining their bodies and enhancing the intimate contact. Her fingers roamed over his biceps, squeezing and massaging the muscles.

He leaned down and kissed her with a thoroughness meant to leave her breathless. It worked. He found her flushed as he watched her take her lower lips between her teeth. He kissed the drop of perspiration between her breasts as he slowly eased off her.

The dress came off and was tossed mindlessly to the floor. Dylan stood and removed what was left of his clothing, his eyes remaining on her all the while. The sight of her wide-eyed admiration filled him with arrogant pride as he joined her on the bed.

He lay beside her, her head resting in the cradle of his arm. He allowed his hand to rest on her abdomen. The heat of her skin nearly scorched him, and she tried to turn toward him.

"Don't," he said gently as he allowed his fingers to toy with the lacy top of her panties.

He could feel the small shivers of anticipation surge through her each time his fingertip slipped beneath the silk. He nuzzled her neck as the exploration continued. He called on all his control as he discovered every delicate inch of her body. Finally, when he could no longer bear the sweet agony, he whisked the panties off and positioned himself between her legs.

Shelby closed her eyes and lifted her willing body toward him. Dylan remained poised above her, but his lips found hers. The deep, demanding kiss lasted for several mind-shattering minutes. He lifted his head and said, "Open your eyes. I want to see your eyes when it happens."

Shelby complied, and he nearly dissolved when he saw his own searing heat mirrored in her expression. He thrust himself into her with slow, tender movements. He felt her nails dig into his shoulders as his body filled her. Together, they fell into the primitive rhythm. He felt her body building toward release as he increased the cadence of their lovemaking. When he at last felt the convulsions of her body around him he allowed himself to savor his own release.

SHELBY LAY watching the blades of the paddle fan spin above her. A myriad of emotions coursed through her mind. How could she have let this happen again? Guilt nudged at her conscience. How could she do this when her baby was missing?

"Is this a guilty silence?" Dylan's soft voice floated through the darkening room.

"A little," she admitted. "I... My son..."

"Don't," he said. He gathered her against him, gently stroking her hair as she rested against his chest.

She could feel the even beat of his heart against her cheek as her hand instinctively rested in the thick mat of hair on his chest. "I've felt so alone since Chad was taken. I guess that's the only explanation for the way I behaved."

"It doesn't matter why we made love."

"Yes, it does." She was arguing more with herself than with him. "What kind of mother spends the afternoon in a hotel room with a man when her baby is missing?"

"One who needs comfort," he answered softly. "This has nothing to do with your love for your son, Shelby."

"I should be out there looking for him," she said as she shrugged away from his hold. She felt alone the moment his hands left her body. And she wasn't all convinced this little fall from grace was just the result of some need to be comforted.

That thought followed her into the bathroom. While she waited for the tub to fill, she stared at her image in the mirror. "Comfort?" she repeated, trying the excuse on her reflection. She frowned. "Complete loss of mental faculties?" She frowned again. "I'm still in love with him," she whispered. Then she nodded.

The long soak in the tub gave her enough time to banish the ghosts of her past. There would be time enough to sort through this mess when she had her son back. By the time she emerged, an artificial smile planted on her face, Shelby showed no outward signs of her inner turmoil.

Nor did Dylan show any signs of inner turmoil. He was seated on the balcony, his bare feet crossed leisurely on the railing. A bottle of beer dangled between his thumb and forefinger.

He turned when he heard her approach. His blue-gray eyes held just a glimmer of sadness that his faint smile couldn't hide. "There's all sorts of drinks and stuff in that cabinet next to the bed."

Shelby shook her head and said, "No, thanks. I'm not really thirsty."

"Jay called while you were in the tub."

"You didn't tell him—"

One of Dylan's brows arched reprovingly. "He's my boss, but I don't report everything."

"I just didn't want him to..." She allowed her voice to trail off.

"He's got three possibles on the car."

Her expression brightened, and she felt that familiar pang of hope swell in her chest. "Are we going to go see them?"

"Not we," he told her. "Me."

"But, Dylan!"

"But nothing," he said, then took a swallow of beer. "I called Rose. She's going to come out here and stay with you while I check things out."

Immediately her head turned to the bed. A blush crept up her cheeks when she realized that he had already taken care of the disheveled covers.

"But if you find him?"

"You'll be the first one to know."

There was an unmistakable tension in the room. Dylan's movements were measured and stiff. And he wouldn't look her in the eye. The knowledge brought the recent memory of their lovemaking to the forefront.

I want to see your eyes when it happens.

She stepped back into the room and found her waterlogged purse. Her wallet was limp, and her checks were damp, but she did manage to convince her ballpoint to work after a bit of coaxing.

"Here," she said, holding the check out to him.

"What's this?"

"For my clothes, and half the cost of the room."

His expression grew dark. "Forget it."

"C'mon, Dylan. There's no reason for you to pay—"

"I'm not destitute, Shelby."

"Neither am I," she countered haughtily.

"No," he admitted as he took another pull on the beer. "But I know you've got most of your money tied up in the Rose Tattoo."

"That doesn't mean I can't afford basic living expenses." She placed the check on the edge of the chair. "We're actually doing okay," she rambled on. "The restaurant business is a lot different from what I used to do, but Rose and I are turning a profit. We've even hired an extra waitress to help on the days Tory is in class."

His brow creased in a series of etched lines. "Tory has day classes?"

"Twice a week," she explained. "She was going to sit this term out, but Rose and I convinced her to keep going."

"How'd you do that?"

His expression was hard, almost angry.

"She didn't have enough for tuition. Rose and I scraped together the difference."

"That's interesting."

"Why?"

"According to Oglethorpe College, Tory Conway isn't registered this quarter."

Chapter Seventeen

"What happened?"

Shelby shifted uncomfortably in the seat, beneath Rose's prodding eyes. "I don't know what you mean."

Rose grunted disbelievingly before gunning her car out of the parking lot. "Something happened. We were supposed to wait back at the inn."

"Well, we didn't. And nothing happened. Not really."

"Really," Rose said. "Tanner looked fit to be tied, and you—" she threw her hands up in the air for an instant "—you have that same look my son had when I caught him stealing a pack of gum from the Piggly Wiggly."

"I didn't steal any gum," Shelby said miserably. Irritably she shoved her hair off her forehead. "I made a terrible mistake."

"By not leveling with him about Chad?"

A heavy sigh escaped past her lips. "Among other things."

"You sleep with him again?"

"Rose!" she bellowed.

"That's a yes."

"I can't believe I could be so stupid again."

Rose jolted the car to a halt at a stoplight and turned in her seat. "You aren't being too objective about this."

"Oh, I'm objective," Shelby groaned. "I'm supposed to be looking for my son, but instead I...I..."

"You sought comfort from the man you love."

Shelby's eyes grew wide, and she was grateful for the shroud of darkness inside the car. "Don't be ridiculous. I can't love Dylan. We have nothing in common. We're practically strangers, for heaven's sake."

"Strangers who made a beautiful baby together."

"You don't understand," Shelby protested.

"So explain it to me."

Wringing her hands, Shelby clamped her eyed shut briefly before beginning. "Dylan and I have this *thing*. It's so powerful, so consuming. It's like no matter what's happening around us, nothing matters but this...this..."

"Passion?"

The word brought with it the image of Dylan's handsome face at the very instant...

"I suppose." Shelby cracked the window. It had suddenly grown very warm inside the car.

"You're lucky," Rose commented after a brief, contemplative silence. "A lot of us go through life never finding that passion. You'd be a fool to walk away from it."

"It's sex, Rose. Dylan has never said he wanted anything more from me."

"Did you ever ask?"

"Ask?"

"You know." Rose waved her heavily jeweled hand in a circular motion. "Did you ever think to give the guy the benefit of the doubt? Maybe he's in love with you, too."

"I never said I was in love with him."

"And my hair's naturally blond," Rose said. "I know you, Shelby. You wouldn't have slept with the guy if you didn't have some strong feelings for him."

"But it's more complicated than that!"

"Because of Chad?"

"Among other things."

"I imagine Tanner will be a mite miffed when he first finds out he's that baby's father. But I think he'll warm up to the notion without a hitch."

"Right," Shelby said with a sneer. "Then what? Dylan once told me he couldn't imagine having a wife and family in his line of work. He even broke an engagement because of his feelings. And then there's the touchy matter of Ned."

"What's Nichols got to do with all this?" Rose queried.

"Dylan hates him."

"If the guy is running guns, he ought to. You, too, for that matter."

"I know I should," Shelby murmured. "But I owe Ned."

"Owe him?" Rose grunted, her disagreement apparent. "The man gave you a job, one you were right good at, I hear. Seems to me that's payment enough."

"But I need Ned," Shelby countered in a barely audible voice.

"I think you need Dylan more."

"But he doesn't need me."

"We'll see," Rose said, allowing those words to hang in the air between them for the remainder of the ride.

The Rose Tattoo was nearly empty when they arrived. Only a few tables were occupied by late-night diners. *Couples,* Shelby noted with distaste. Normal couples who didn't have secrets.

"Hey, Shelby," Keith called as she and Rose weaved their way through the kitchen. "Any news?"

Sadly Shelby shook her head. "Not yet."

"Anything I can do?"

The question came from Tory. Shelby stared at the young woman, her mind replaying Dylan's startling revelation.

"You can come up to my office," Shelby said. Then, turning to Rose, she added, "Give us a few minutes, will you?"

"I'm outa here," Rose announced. "Unless you want me to stay with you?"

"No," Shelby said, managing a small smile. "Thanks for picking me up."

"Think about what I said, Shelby. Ask Tanner what he wants. His answers might surprise you."

"Maybe," Shelby hedged.

USING THE MAP provided by the rent-a-cop at the gate, Dylan turned into a horseshoe-shaped drive in front of a huge house bathed in diffused light from a row of flood lamps. The muted sound of a small dog's yapping greeted him when he stepped onto the crushed-stone pavement.

Taking the steps two at a time, he rammed his shirt into the waistband of his pants and pressed the doorbell. Plastering a pleasant expression on his face, he let out a breath as he waited. He wasn't expecting this visit to be any more informative than the two that had preceded it.

A small white dog and a small white-haired woman peered out from a small crack in the door.

"Yes?"

Flipping open his wallet, Dylan offered his identification, as well as an introduction. "Are you Mrs. Carstairs?"

Surprise lifted her dark brows toward the mass of white-blue curls. "Yes."

He repeated the drill, asking if she owned a car like the one he was looking for, then asking to see it.

"Come in," she said tentatively as she scooped up the yapping dog and cradled it under her arm. The dog's black eyes watched him from beneath a crisp blue ribbon.

Dylan sneered at the annoying little creature. Foolish could eat it in one gulp.

Dylan followed the tiny woman through the expansive space, trying to figure out what such a small woman needed with so much room. It wasn't a house, it was a showplace. He could only imagine his mother's reaction to a place this size— *Too much to keep clean.*

"This way," she instructed as she led him through the kitchen.

Flipping a switch, she filled the garage with light. The black Taurus was parked next to a sleek white Mercedes, and there was still ample room for a third vehicle. In fact, he thought with a snide smile, the garage was bigger than his apartment.

Working his way past a collection of bikes, Dylan checked the condition of the car, not expecting to find anything of consequence. He was right.

"Can you tell me what this is all about?" Mrs. Carstairs called from her perch on the steps. The dog whined, as well.

"I'm trying to find a car matching this description that *may* have been on the island yesterday."

"Oh, it was here," Mrs. Carstairs said with conviction.

Dylan straightened and tried to keep his surprise in check. "There are two other cars like yours on the island."

"Rebecca's and Grace's," she affirmed. "It wasn't one of theirs."

"How do you know there was a fourth car on the island?" he questioned skeptically.

"Angel," she said simply.

"Come again?" Dylan asked, feeling his hope dissipate as he regarded his elderly informant.

"Angel," she said more forcefully, holding the dog out and allowing it to dangle like a squirming dustball. "We were up at the straw market, and Angel took me to the wrong car."

Great, he thought disgustedly. His informant was a pedigreed pile of groomed white hair. "Explain what happened."

"I parked at the market, and when we came back, Angel and I went to the wrong car. It wasn't until I tried my key and set off the car alarm that I realized I'd made a mistake."

Dylan moved with such swiftness that the dog dived for protection beneath one of the cars. "I take it the owner came out?"

"Sure," Mrs. Carstairs said, a faint stain creeping up her thin neck. "She was quite nice about the whole ordeal."

"Did you get her name?"

Mrs. Carstairs sighed and began to stroke her chin with age-gnarled fingers. "I believe I did. Let's see. I know she called the baby Chad—"

"She had a baby with her?"

"Cute little thing, too," Mrs. Carstairs said with a fond smile. "And her name was Katherine, I think. Yes. Katherine."

"Katherine what?" Dylan thundered. Mrs. Carstairs jolted at his tone, and Dylan uttered some sort of apology. "Did you happen to catch her last name?"

Mrs. Carstairs shook her head. "Afraid not."

"Tell me what she looked like."

"She was a handsome woman. Average height, fair complexion. Her hair was brown, as were her eyes."

"Anything else?" Dylan asked as he scribbled furiously in his notebook. "Anything you can recall that struck you about this woman?"

"Aside from her grandson, you mean?"

Dylan's nod was stiffened by the overwhelming anger boiling in his blood.

"She said she was glad the car alarm had gone off, because she had lost track of time."

"Time for what?"

"She had to hurry back into town for a meeting."

"What kind of a meeting? Did she say?"

Mrs. Carstairs's shoulders slouched forward. "Some society or another. I'm sorry, I just can't recall."

Jabbing the notebook between his teeth, Dylan extracted one of his cards from his wallet and handed it to her. "Please call me if you remember anything," he said.

He couldn't wait to get back to Charleston. Back to Shelby. He finally had concrete information about her son.

TORY'S SOFT FOOTSTEPS followed her up the steps and down the corridor. Shelby wasn't exactly sure how she would handle the situation, even as she took her position of authority behind the cluttered desk.

Any thoughts she might have entertained about Dylan being mistaken about Tory were erased when she looked at the nervous woman seated across from her. Tory's blue eyes were as big as the saucers she carted around. Her lower lip trembled, as did the small hand tugging on the short hairs at the nape of her neck.

"I need—"

"Wait!" Tory jumped to her feet, interrupting her. "I know what this is all about."

"Really?" Shelby tried to remain calm, tried to keep the disappointment out of her expression.

"The money." Tory barely managed to get the words out. "I know you and Rose meant for me to use it for school."

"That was our understanding."

"I was going to," Tory insisted, moving forward so that her hands rested, palms down, on the desk. Several papers fluttered on the breeze created by her sudden movement.

"Something came up, and I needed to use the money for something else."

"Are you in trouble?" Shelby asked.

"Trouble?" Tory blinked. "Oh, you mean like you were?"

Shelby winced, but didn't completely lose her grip on her self-control.

"I didn't mean it like that," Tory explained on a rush of mint-scented breath. "I didn't mean to insinuate there was anything wrong—"

Shelby lifted her hand. "It's okay, Tory."

The other woman fell silent as she slumped back into the chair. Shelby regarded her for a long moment before speaking. "Whoever has Chad wants one hundred thousand dollars."

Tory's gasp was audible. Her shocked expression dissolved, and was replaced by one Shelby could only categorize as a look of horror.

"You don't think I'm involved?"

"That's a lot of money, Tory. And if you're in financial trouble . . ." her voice trailed off.

"God!" Tory exclaimed, raking a hand through her short hair. "I could never do anything to hurt Chad. I can't believe you would even think I was capable of such a thing."

"Then explain to me what you did with the money Rose and I gave you for your tuition."

Tory surprised her by meeting her eyes squarely. "I gave the entire thirty-five hundred dollars to the Ashley Villas Rest Home."

"Ashley Villas?"

"My mother," Tory said softly. "She hasn't been, well, right since my daddy left us. She had a breakdown and never really recovered."

"I'm sorry," Shelby said feelingly. "When did all this happen? And why didn't you tell us?"

"Fifteen years ago."

Shelby's shock must have registered on her face, because Tory continued.

"Daddy used to own this place."

"The Tattoo?" Shelby queried.

Tory nodded and said, "This used to be my parents' bedroom." She punctuated the statement with a sweeping arc of her hand. "Of course, this was before Charleston became such a touristy place. When Daddy owned it, it was a townie bar. Kind of rough."

"And your mother?"

"Mama cooked burgers, served drinks and cleaned."

"And your father left?"

Tory's nod was a bit stiffer this time. "I was only eight. But he basically cleaned out the accounts and took off."

"And your mother couldn't handle it?"

"Nope. Daddy broke her heart and her spirit. She never recovered."

"If you were only eight . . ."

"My grandmother helped out," Tory said with a re-membering smile. "Gran took real good care of my mama. Me, too. But she passed away two years ago."

"So now you're responsible for your mother's care?"

Tory sighed and clasped her hands behind her head. Her eyes went wistfully to the ceiling. "I don't seem to be as good at caring for Mama as Gran was. She's been going downhill ever since Gran died. But Ashley Villas is a great place for her. She's safe there."

"Safe?"

"Mama has it in her head that she doesn't want to live without Daddy."

Shelby felt a swell of compassion fill her chest. "Why didn't you say something, Tory? We would have done more."

"People don't usually take too kindly to the notion that you've got mental illness in your family." Tory's smile be-came wry. "I guess they think it's catching or some-thing."

Shelby's expression matched her companion's as she recalled the way her neighbors had shunned her because she was an unwed mother. "How are things now?"

"Okay," she said with a shrug. "But it seems to me you have enough troubles of your own without worrying about mine." Tory leaned forward, her round face stiff with concern. "Where are you going to get the money to pay the ransom?"

Shelby sucked in a breath. "I'm working on it."

"I might be able to get some of the money back from the rest home—"

"Don't be silly," Shelby told her. "Thirty-five hundred wouldn't even make a dent, and besides—" she reached over the desk and patted Tory's hand "—maybe Dylan will find him first."

"Dylan? The guy who keeps coming by here, asking questions?"

Shelby nodded.

"He's Chad's father, isn't he?"

Shelby felt as if someone had kicked her in the stomach. "Why—"

"Chad looks just like him," Tory said sheepishly. "It's the eyes. Those vivid gray-blues are a dead giveaway."

"You didn't say anything to Dylan?"

Tory's pale brows drew together in a frown. "No. Are you telling me that he doesn't know? Is the guy blind?"

"He's never seen Chad," Shelby admitted.

Tory shook her head in utter disbelief. "I don't think you'll be able to keep your secret when he sees him."

"If he does," Shelby said, as pain gripped her chest.

"When," Tory insisted, coming around the desk and giving Shelby a much needed hug. "He'll be back in no time. You'll see."

"I hope so," Shelby groaned in a tight voice.

After soliciting Tory's promise that she would say nothing about the ransom demand, Shelby sat alone in her office. It was nearly two in the morning when she stepped over to the window. It was a black, starless night that seemed to mirror her bleak feelings of despair. Fingering the edge of the curtain, she closed her eyes and tried to envision her son, safe and sleeping in some unknown place. Warm, silent tears spilled over her cheeks. Anguish threatened to consume her.

"Shelby?"

Spinning away from the window, she found Keith lingering in the doorway, his head downcast.

"You okay?"

"Thanks, Keith. I'm all right."

"You don't look all right."

"I'm fine," she insisted as she dried her face with the backs of her hands.

"I was going to head out, but if you need someone to—"

"Go," she said with a forced smile. "I'm just going to do a little paperwork."

"I'm sure that stuff can wait."

"But I can't," she admitted softly. "I'll just work until I can't see straight."

"You sure?"

Shelby nodded and went over to him to give him a gentle nudge out the door. She listened until she heard the sound of his car starting. Wandering down to the kitchen, she frowned when she noted the metal pans stacked in the sink. Rose would have a fit in the morning, one she would assuredly share with Keith.

Tugging opened the refrigerator, Shelby grabbed a bowl of sliced fruits and then collected a fork. She wasn't hungry, but she had the beginnings of a headache. Maybe some nourishment would keep it in check until she could exhaust her body enough to garner a few precious hours of sleep.

The dining room was a neat arrangement of tables with chairs perched on top. Josh and Tory had no doubt seen to it that this area of the building was ready for the next day's lunch crowd. Going to the jukebox, Shelby selected from the few non-Elvis offerings. Reaching behind the machine, she cranked up the volume so that she would be able to hear the music from her office.

With the fruit in her hand, she lumbered up the steps, the sound muffled by the music. "Exhaust the mind, exhaust the body," she told herself, repeating the words her mother often said.

The stack of mail, invoices and bills on the corner of her desk was moved onto the blotter in front of her. Using her fingernail, Shelby slit open the first envelope as she popped a strawberry into her mouth. She glanced over the text of the letter briefly before tossing it into the wastepaper basket. They didn't need any aluminum siding, even at half price.

She was in the act of reaching for the next item when the corner of one of the envelopes buried in the pile took her breath away. Carefully she eased it out.

CHAD'S MOM.

Ripping into it, she scanned the bold, concise block printing.

THE RULES HAVE CHANGED. BRING THE MONEY TO WATERFRONT PARK TOMORROW AT 9:00 A.M. SHARP. NO COPS OR CHAD DIES.

Shelby closed her eyes and took deep, purposeful breaths in an attempt to quell her panic. *Think!* her mind demanded. But there really was only one thing she could do.

Glancing at her watch, she grabbed the phone and dialed. Her toe tapped impatiently as she went through the process of placing an international call.

"Is this Mr. Chan?" she asked the semifamiliar voice.

"It is."

"This is Shelby Hunnicutt. We spoke yesterday. I need to speak to Mr. Nichols immediately. It's urgent."

"I'm sorry, Miss Hunnicutt. Mr. Nichols has checked out."

"Checked out?" she gasped. "How can I reach him?"

"I believe you should try the American State Department."

"Whatever for?"

"He was taken into their custody by the Turkish police earlier today."

"Why?" she yelled into the receiver. "Why would they be holding Ned?"

"Because I told them to."

Shelby's eyes collided with the angry, restrained figure of Dylan Tanner looming in the doorway.

Chapter Eighteen

"You?" Shelby gulped.

"Miss Hunnicutt?" Mr. Chan called into the receiver.

"Never mind," Shelby said dully as she placed the phone back on the cradle.

Dylan strode into the room, reaching her in three thundering strides. His expression was hard, and his eyes were unforgiving. Menace fairly radiated from his large body as he loomed above her.

Shelby could feel his harsh breath wash across her face from between his tightly clenched teeth. She couldn't let him intimidate, not now. Too much was at stake.

"You'll have to do something to have him released," she told him.

Dylan grabbed her from the chair, his fingers painfully pinching the skin at her upper arms. "I can't believe you," he growled. "You've made quite a habit out of sleeping with me and then running to Nichols. What gives?"

Shelby looked into those angry silver slits, and her own eyes narrowed in response. "Let me go, Dylan. You're hurting me."

His eyes traveled to where his fingers bit into her flesh. Instantly his grip loosened, though he didn't release her. "Why?" he asked. It was a single strangled syllable.

"I need Ned's help."

"You think your gunrunning ex-lover is better equipped than I am to find your son?"

"No," she told him honestly. "And he isn't my ex-lover."

"Great!" he said, his voice grating. "It's still going on? What's the matter, Shelby—having trouble choosing between the two of us?"

"It isn't what you think," she insisted, trying vainly to twist away from him.

"I don't know," he told her, derision hanging on each word. "Seems to me you must get some sort of cheap thrill playing both ends against the middle."

"Stop it! You don't know what you're talking about."

"Then enlighten me," he said challengingly. "But I should tell you, I just came from seeing Jay. He played the tape for me."

"Tape?"

"Your heartwarming phone call to Nichols yesterday. You should have known better than to call him from your bedroom, Shelby. Not too bright."

"Jay knows?" she asked.

He nodded as his eyes roamed over her face, quietly studying the apparently visible signs of her fear. "Why would you ask Nichols?"

"I want your promise that you won't tell Jay."

He snorted. "No way."

"Then let go of me, and do whatever you have to for Ned to be released."

"Why should I?"

"Because if you don't, they'll kill my son."

Dylan's hands slid up and down her arms. She could almost see him thinking, hear the litany of arguments she felt sure were echoing through his brain. Soundlessly he stepped away from her, offering her his broad back as he stood at the window.

"Dylan?"

"Be quiet for a minute," he said in a hoarse voice.

Shelby stared at his back for what felt like an eternity. The music had stopped—not that she could have heard it above the pounding of her heart. Trepidation began a slow ascent up her spine, until it threatened total domination.

"Nichols isn't your lover."

It was a statement, not a question.

"No."

"Never has been, has he?"

It was a question, and an accusation.

"No."

Dylan's turn was slow, deliberate, measured. Shelby held her breath, bracing against the unknown. His eyes moved between Shelby and the framed photograph of the baby, his fists opening and closing at his sides.

Anxiously she watched the play of emotions in his eyes as the truth stretched between them like a wire. Dylan laughed harshly.

"He's mine." He said the words in a voice Shelby had never heard before. It was sarcastic, and very, very angry.

No longer able to stand the intense scrutiny of his penetrating eyes, she lowered her head and felt the burn of impending tears. She waited for the explosion. She reached for him with a beseeching hand. One he shrugged away from as if her touch were as repulsive as her lies. A sneering smirk marred his features as he stepped over to the bar and poured himself a glass of Scotch from the dusty bottle.

His mouth thinned as he swallowed the contents in one long drink. She could see the muscles of his jaw working as he ground his teeth. The silence became a deafening madness that felt as if it could go on forever.

"I never meant for—"

Dylan held up one hand to cut off her words while he poured himself another drink. "I had a feeling you were keeping a secret," he began, in a dangerously calm voice. "I just never dreamed it would have anything to do with me."

"I can explain, Dylan."

"Really?" he shot back, slamming the glass down in a thundering punctuation. "Can *you* explain why you decided to deprive me of the first year of my own son's life? Or maybe *you* can explain why you didn't tell me you were pregnant? Or maybe you've got some explanation for the way you've behaved since the night *our* son was taken." Dylan took two steps closer, but Shelby was having a difficult time seeing him through the glistening of unshed tears. "Now we've wasted God knows how many man-hours hunting for Nichols, when we could have been searching for Chad. If something's—"

"Don't say it!" Shelby screamed. Her head dropped, and she felt her whole body shaking with each gut-wrenching sob. "Please, Dylan..." she pleaded in a near whisper.

She fully expected him to storm from the house. Instead, she felt herself being dragged against him. She drank in the scent of his skin, but didn't react. Not until Dylan began to gently stroke his hand through her hair.

"Why didn't you tell me?" His voice was softer, calmer, but still held a slight edge.

Shelby went rigid in his arms, not certain she was capable of dealing with his recriminations. "The usual reasons."

"Being?"

His hand moved to her waist, his fingers kneading the tight muscles at the small of her back.

"I wasn't sure how you'd react. You'd already told me you didn't want a family. Not in your line of work."

"No," he said as his hands cupped her face, tilting it toward his. "I told you I broke my engagement because I wasn't ready for a family then. It was ten years ago, Shelby. You didn't listen."

His thumbs wiped away her tears, and his eyes held hers.

"I'm sorry. If what you said is true, I may have cost my baby his life—"

"Hush," he said as he brushed a kiss against her lips. "I was angry, Shelby. I shouldn't have said that."

"But do you think it's possible? How will I live with myself if I've done anything to jeopardize Chad?"

"You haven't done anything," Dylan insisted.

"I'm sorry about all the lies."

"I'm not thrilled that you didn't trust me enough to come to me. I'm sorry I missed the first nine months of my son's life."

"I never meant—"

"For me to find out," he finished with a sad smile. "But I have, so we go from here."

"Go where?"

"We'll figure that out after we get Chad home."

Shelby reached up and grabbed a handful of his shirt. "You won't take him away from me, will you?"

"What kind of a man do you think I am?" His laugh was even sadder than his smile. "Of course not, Shelby. Give me some credit for being a decent guy."

"I do," she told him.

"Then explain all of it to me," Dylan suggested as he stepped back and leaned against her desk. "What's with you and Nichols? And when did the kidnapper contact you?"

"When we were searching Market Street for the woman and the baby. He called me on the cellular and set it up."

"What's the plan this time?"

Reaching behind him, Shelby tugged the ominous letter from the desk and handed it to him. He scanned the copy, a definite frown curving the corners of his mouth downward. She could almost feel the anger radiating from his large body.

"You can't tell Jay," Shelby said imploringly. "He'll kill Chad if the authorities are involved."

"Jay can—"

"I'm not willing to risk it," she told him as she moved to stand in front of him. They stood toe-to-toe, with Shelby craning her neck to meet his eyes. "Promise me, Dylan. Promise me."

"You don't ask for much, do you?"

"I can't risk my son's safety."

"My son, too."

"WE HAVEN'T SOLVED the problem of the money," Shelby told him as they entered her house.

"No," he agreed as his hand reached back for hers. "We haven't."

"You have to let me talk to Ned."

His hand tightened an instant before the rest of his body steeled in reaction to her statement. He pulled her in the direction of the living room.

After depositing her on the sofa, Dylan found the switch on the lamp. Soft light illuminated his features. Shelby felt the pangs of anxiety returning as she peered up into his troubled face. Shelby had the distinct impression that he was battling his temper. He hadn't managed to keep that spark of annoyance out of his glistening eyes.

"Tell me the rest of your secrets, Shelby." His voice was subdued, dangerously so. "Tell me why you left me and went running to Nichols. Especially when you knew you were going to have my baby."

"I—"

The shrill ring of the telephone prevented her answering. Automatically she reached over and grabbed the receiver.

"Hello?"

"Miss Hunnicutt?"

"Yes. Who is this?"

"Kurt Mitchell from down the street."

"Yes, Mr. Mitchell?"

"I know all about your little boy, and I just thought you'd want to know—"

"Yes?"

"That black car I saw on the night of the kidnapping?"

"Yes?"

"I'm pretty sure it's parked out front of my house."

"Thank you," Shelby managed to say before she hung up and filled Dylan in.

"Call 911. Tell them to come in quiet."

"Where are you going?" she wailed. Her eyes were fixed on the lethal-looking gun he now held in his right hand.

"I'll go check out our friend."

"Can't you wait for the police?"

Dylan looked down to where she had a death grip on his arm. His smile was slow and genuine. "I guess this means that you really care, huh?"

Her cheeks burned as she watched him leave. She tried to keep him in sight through the window as she called the emergency dispatcher. Dylan bobbed behind trees, slunk behind cars, until she could no longer see him in the hazy light of the street lamps.

Propping herself on her knees, she carefully put back the curtains and repeated, "Come on," as if it were a mantra. She could see no movement on the street, nothing to calm her growing concerns for his safety. Minutes passed like years, and she moved only when the painful tingling in her legs demanded it.

She paced. She prayed. She even cursed as she waited, feeling helpless and useless. "Don't let anything happen to him," she said in a whisper. If something happened to Dylan...

Her grim thoughts were blissfully halted by a loud and sudden disturbance moving toward the house. Shelby ran to the door and threw it open.

Dylan was dragging a struggling man up the sidewalk, flanked by a small group of police officers. Porch lights blinked on in a choreographed display of overt curiosity.

"Keith?" she gasped when she saw the culprit.

"None other," Dylan rasped, sounding winded and heartily annoyed.

He gave the smaller man a shove, so that Keith tumbled into the foyer with a thud. "Hey!"

"Thanks, guys," Dylan said as he slammed the door on the other men.

Instinctively Shelby stood behind him, peering around his shoulders as Keith slowly dragged himself to his feet.

"What are you doing?" she asked.

"Good question," Dylan added sarcastically.

"Just—watching out for you," Keith stammered, wiping his hands on the front of his pants.

"Peeping out for you is probably closer to the truth."

The two men glowered at one another.

"I'm not a pervert," Keith insisted.

"Then what have you been doing slinking though the neighborhood?" Dylan challenged.

"I was just looking out for her. With her kid snatched—"

"Wrong answer." Sneering, Dylan moved swiftly, anchoring Keith to the wall, his forearm against the smaller man's throat.

"Dylan!"

"We know you were out there the night Chad was taken," Dylan said.

"Keith," Shelby said imploringly. "Is that true? Were you here that night?"

His Adam's apple flickered just above Dylan's forearm. "I was parked down the street."

His evasive response earned him additional pressure from his captor. Shelby stepped forward and placed her hand on Dylan. Keith looked on the verge of collapse. "If you strangle him, he can't tell us anything."

Dylan snarled once, then loosened his hold. "Make it good, Keith."

"I was on the side, by the hedges."

"And?"

"And when I heard footsteps, I bolted."

"What footsteps?" Shelby nearly screamed. "Why didn't you tell me this before?"

"Because," Dylan began as he slowly released Keith, "then he would have had to admit that he's been staking you out for some time. Isn't that right?"

"I just wanted to be close to you," he said, in a pathetically soft voice. "I would never do anything to hurt you, Shelby. Chad, neither."

Shelby fell against the cool surface of the wall. "I know that," she managed to say.

"And if I'd really seen anything, I'd have told. Honest."

"What *did* you see?" Dylan asked as he stepped next to Shelby and placed his hand possessively at her waist.

The contact was enough to short-circuit her frazzled nerves. She could feel every inch of his fingers through the fabric of her dress. She was aware of the warmth of his body where it brushed hers. She was losing her grip!

"I only glanced back for maybe a second. There was this guy with a ladder coming through the back."

"What did he look like?"

Keith shrugged, glanced at Dylan and said, "Like you."

LIKE YOU. Dylan played the answer in his mind long after that little weasel left. He frowned, wondering why he had allowed Shelby to talk him in to letting the guy walk out of here. Keith and his little infatuation might seem harmless to her, but he knew better. He'd come across a few crazies in his time, and Keith had the makings of a true delusional.

"I could have fixed you something," Shelby said as she joined him in the kitchen.

His heart jumped to his throat when he saw the incredibly sexy little robe belted at her even sexier waist. He thought about bending her over the kitchen table. As much as he liked the idea, he knew it wouldn't solve anything. In fact, he was fast realizing that their strong physical attraction was one thing that seemed to scare Shelby into secrecy.

"Peanut butter on a piece of bread," he said, holding it up for her inspection. "Hardly an imposition on my limited culinary expertise."

She sat down in the chair and crossed her legs. The robe covered less than half of her shapely thighs, and Dylan nearly groaned when he allowed his eyes to caress the tanned skin. He had that same curious, guilty feeling he'd had in the eighth grade, when Marybeth Bartoli had gotten a conduct referral from the sisters from wearing her uniform too short.

"Is something wrong?"

Yes. "No," he assured her.

He watched as she lifted a bottle of water to her lips. His eyes remained fixed as she wrapped her rosy lips around the top of the bottle. He followed the path of the water, down her slender throat, down toward the deep V where the edges of the robe met. He could just make out the gentle swell of her breast—

"Dylan!" she said sharply.

"Sorry," he mumbled.

"We need to do something about the payoff. You have to get Ned to a phone, so I can talk to him."

The pleasant diversion of ogling her body evaporated under the instant steam of his temper. He didn't want any part of Nichols.

"You heard Keith. He said the guy looked like me. Nichols and I are similar in height and coloring."

"Ned does not have my son."

"Our son," he said deliberately. "And I'm not as convinced as you seem to be."

"Then just trust me on this."

"You tell me why you're so sure Nichols doesn't have the baby, and I'll let it rest."

He watched her expression falter. Saw the flash of uncertainty cloud her clear blue eyes. "Can't you just take my word for it?"

"Not without some rational explanation for your blind faith in that slimeball."

"He isn't a slimeball," she countered, crossing her arms defiantly in front of her small body.

"What would you call him?" Dylan taunted.

"My father."

Chapter Nineteen

He was alone in the kitchen. Shelby had left just after delivering her latest little bomb. It explained a lot, but left him with a whole slew of new questions. After discarding his half-eaten sandwich in the garbage, Dylan ran his fingers through his hair and let out a deep breath.

"It's family day at the Hunnicutt house," he grumbled. Learning he was Chad's father had brought with it a whole host of wonderful emotions. Finding out Nichols was Shelby's father made him want to spit.

He thought back to their conversation on the beach. She certainly hadn't grown up with Nichols in the picture. He wondered what rock the guy had crawled out from under to stake his fatherly claim. And why.

That ominous thought followed him up the stairs. He stopped outside Shelby's door, listening for sounds. He remained there for several minutes, debating. Finally emotion overruled common sense, and he grasped the knob.

"Dylan?" She said the name in the dark.

"I just wanted to make sure you were okay."

"I'm fine."

He could tell that was a lie. He could almost hear the tears in her husky voice, and he felt a surge of protectiveness surge up from deep inside his soul.

Slowly he walked to the edge of the bed. The room smelled faintly feminine, just like Shelby. Cautiously he took a seat, feeling her body move toward his weight.

He wanted to hold her, comfort her. He settled for ramming his fists in the pockets of his shorts.

"You don't sound fine."

"I'm scared."

"I know," he agreed on a breath. "I am, too."

"What if we don't get him back. What if—"

"I'll find him, Shelby. I promise you."

The room was silent, except for the occasional sound of her shifting beneath the covers. That inspired vivid memories of their passionate afternoon. He licked his lips, remembering the taste of her mouth.

"You'll like him," she said softly.

"I know I will," Dylan agreed. He wished he could see her face. "I'm sure you've done a great job with him."

"After seeing you with Keith, I know where he gets his violent streak."

"I'm not violent."

"Tell Keith that," Shelby said.

"I'd like to tattoo it across his forehead with an oyster fork."

"No, you're not violent," she said, teasingly. "Wonder how I ever got that impression?"

"When did you find out Nichols was your father?"

"The same day I discovered I was pregnant."

Hanging his head, Dylan sucked in air.

"The same day you told me you needed my testimony to put Ned in jail for the rest of his life."

The knot in his gut twisted and festered. "No wonder you bailed out."

"I didn't bail out," she said, after apparently giving his statement some consideration. "I just wasn't interested in letting the two of you tear me apart like two dogs going after the same bone."

"I wouldn't have pressured you, Shelby."

"We'll never know."

"What about Nichols? Did he back off?"

He heard a small decisive sound from the bed. "Ned was furious when I told him I wanted out. He didn't let up for a long time. That's probably why Chad was born a month early. My blood pressure went through the roof."

"I hope he rots in hell."

"He has basically the same wish for you."

"Then why didn't you help me put him away?"

"I would have," she answered immediately. "Until I realized the truth."

"Which was?"

"That Ned was manipulating me, and so were you."

"I never tried to manipulate you."

"Then how did I end up pregnant?"

Dylan tenuous hold on his self-control vanished. Blindly he reached out with both hands.

"What are you doing?"

"I'm about to show you how you ended up pregnant," he said against her open mouth. "And believe me, it has nothing to do with Nichols."

Despite his rather harsh tone, Dylan took infinite care in finessing her mouth beneath his. He savored, tasted and revered her with his kiss before gently laying her against the pillow. Wordlessly he rose and left her in the dark, silently praying she would see the light.

"WHERE HAVE YOU BEEN?" she demanded as soon as he slipped in the back door.

"Getting this." He held up a tattered gym bag and winked. "One hundred thousand U.S. dollars."

Relief washed over her as she flung herself against his solid chest. He smelled of soap and coffee.

"Where did you get it?"

"I wangled a few favors at the office," he said against her hair.

"You didn't tell anyone?"

Shelby backed up and searched his face. She could tell the deception weighed heavily on him.

"No."

"Thank you," she said as she reached up to trace one of the small lines by his mouth. "I know this is hard for you."

"Let's hope the ends justify the means."

"I should know in about two hours."

"I?"

"He told me to come alone."

"And he'll think you have."

"But last time—"

"Last time I wasn't calling the shots. This time I am."

She was torn between her fierce need for his support and her desire to follow the instructions explicitly. One glance at the tight set of his jaw told her all she needed to know. Short of hog-tying him in the basement, there was no way she could keep Dylan from accompanying her to the park.

"Take this and get going," he instructed.

"What about you?"

"I told you about my conversation with Mrs. Carstairs. We know there are at least two people involved here. I'll follow you in my car, from a safe distance."

With the bag of money in the trunk, Shelby negotiated the rush-hour traffic and arrived at the park a few minutes before nine.

Donning sunglasses, she nervously glanced around before retrieving the payoff from the car. "Now what?" she whispered.

Standing at the edge of the parking area, she scanned the grass and brick sections near the water's edge. A few joggers, a man reading the paper, a few young children—but nothing and no one resembling a kidnapper.

"What do you think he'll look like?" she said to herself. "Fangs and a hairy wart?"

Shelby meandered through the park, her eyes darting from spot to spot behind the shield of her glasses. She hoped for a glimpse of Dylan, then berated herself for the thought. If she spotted him, so might the kidnapper.

Glancing at her watch, she felt the first stirrings of panic. It was after nine. Shelby continued to walk slowly through the park, turning her head every few feet when curiosity and misgivings got the better of her judgment. She ended up at the pier, a walkway out over the muddy waters of the harbor, dotted with graceful white swings hanging every few feet.

She moved along the right side, one hand on the railing, the other tightly closed on the handle of the gym bag. The stale scent of rotting marine life wafted up from the calm brown waters. Stopping briefly, she watched the skeletal remains of a foam container float by.

"Miss?"

Shelby turned toward the child's voice, meeting an expectant pair of brown eyes. The young boy had skin the color of chocolate. His clothes told her instantly that he was from the well-hidden, little-discussed poor section of the city. The part of Charleston that never made it into any of the travel brochures.

"Yes?" she said, as she began to reach into her purse for a few dollars.

"I need the bag."

"Y-you?" she stammered as her mouth fell open.

"The man said to tell you to give me the bag and he'll be in touch."

"But you're just a child."

"Ten next month." He beamed proudly.

"What's your name?"

"The man said that I wasn't supposed to talk to you. Just get the bag."

Shelby closed her eyes and hoped for some sort of divine intervention. It seemed ludicrous to hand such an enormous sum of money to a mere boy.

"If I don't hurry, he won't pay me," the boy said urgently, glancing over one bony shoulder. "I can sure use that ten dollars, ma'am."

Thrusting the bag into his chest, Shelby watched helplessly as he struggled back down the pier under the heavy weight of the money. Every cell in her body screamed for her to follow him, to see if he would lead her to Chad. But the rational side of her brain insisted on some sort of calculated approach. God, she wished Dylan was there.

When the boy rounded the corner of Bay Street, Shelby damned reason and set off after him. Gathering the hem of her cotton skirt in her hand, she jogged through the park, her hair slapping at her back.

She reached Bay and looked right. Nothing. Without debate, she continued to follow the child's route, surveying each alley and driveway along the way.

She stopped short about three blocks from the park, nearly falling on her face when she negotiated an abrupt halt.

"Dylan!" she called.

Running up the uneven alleyway, she reached them, breathless.

Dylan straddled the subdued form of a man beneath the full weight of his body. The man's hands were crossed behind his body, limp, as Dylan slapped shiny metal cuffs on his wrists. Just beyond them, Shelby spotted the young boy, cowering against the wall. His eyes were wide, staring at some remembered violence.

Shelby stepped over Dylan's feet and went to see the boy. "Are you all right?"

He gulped. "Uh-huh."

"He's great," Dylan managed as he wrestled the man to his feet and leaned him against the wall. "Greg was my partner. Right, son?"

"Uh-huh."

"Greg helped me catch the bad guy."

Shelby placed an appreciative hand on the child's shoulder, her eyes fixed on the back of the prisoner's head. "Where's Chad?"

"He was just about to explain that to me," Dylan said as he jerked the man so that his face was visible.

Shelby gasped. "Toby?"

"You know this guy?"

Looking past the trickles of blood from his nose and fast-swelling lip, Shelby nodded. "He's Keith's roommate. Toby Ballentine."

"Keith?" Dylan muttered, adding a few choice expletives. "I knew I should have turned that bozo over to the cops last night. At least now I understand how the guy had all your private telephone numbers."

"He doesn't know about this," Toby said between clenched teeth.

"Where is my son?" Shelby demanded.

He coughed. "I don't know."

Dylan placed his fist strategically in the man's rib cage. "Try again."

"I swear!" Toby yelped, clamping his arms at his sides in anticipation of another blow. "I don't have him."

"You just thought you'd pick up a few extra dollars?" Dylan said next to the man's ear.

"Keith and me were gonna open our own place. Until he started working for her." Toby cast Shelby a hateful look that rocked her in her shoes. "He's so hot for you, he changed his mind about our plan. Said he'd be happy to work for you for the rest of his life."

"You will be, too," Dylan snarled at him, his voice barely audible over the fast-approaching wail of a siren. "Only you'll do it as a guest of the state."

Shelby and Greg sat on the angled curb while Dylan and the local authorities worked out the arrangements to get Toby off the street. Knowing he would be incarcerated was of little consequence. Shelby still didn't have her baby.

"Let's go," Dylan said as he offered his hand.

She noted the knuckles were bruised and slightly swollen, but he didn't seem to notice the injury.

They walked arm in arm, Shelby resting her head against his chest, her hand on his stomach.

"Toby never had Chad, did he?" she asked when he got behind the wheel.

"Nope," Dylan answered. "But we still have the information Mrs. Carstairs gave me."

"Katherine Somebody, who attended a Something Society meeting yesterday?"

His hand shot across the car and captured her chin, forcing her to meet his eyes. "It's a start, Shelby."

"Can we stop at the Tattoo? I want to make sure Rose fires Keith when he shows his face this afternoon."

"I thought you were feeling charitable toward the guy."

"I'm fresh out of charity," she assured him glibly. "Besides, I left the pictures from the videotape in my office."

"We have more."

"I know, but they're close, and I want to memorize that woman's hand so that when I see it, I'll know."

AT ROSE'S INSISTENCE, they were seated in the dining room. They had pushed the plates of half-eaten food off to one side, to lay the pictures out in an arc.

A foot, a hand, and a ring. That was it. But something about the ring seemed oddly familiar to Shelby. She wondered if she hadn't seen the woman. Maybe she even knew the woman holding her son.

"Hi," Tory said as she came rushing into the room, fastening the top button of her blouse. "Rose filled me in. I'm so sorry."

"Thanks," they said in unison.

Tory leaned between them and ran her fingernail over the enlargement of the ring. "Your suspect belongs to the Sisters of History?"

"What?" Dylan bellowed, his massive hand clamped on Tory's wrist.

"Yeah," Tory said, startled. "That's the insignia of the society. Charleston blue bloods, mostly."

"What does this society do?" Shelby asked.

"Have lunch." Tory grunted. "Give out plaques."

"The plaque!" Shelby squealed, recognition dawning. "This is the same design that was on the doors of the homes in the Historic District. The small one beneath the historical markers."

"Right, those," Tory agreed. "And if Dylan would be kind enough to take his vise off my wrist, I'll go get a phone book so you can look these babes up."

"Sorry," Dylan said.

Shelby noted a small stain of red on each of his high cheekbones. "Why would a society matron take my baby?"

Dylan raked his finger through his hair, shaking his head. "I haven't got a clue. But I'm damned sure going to find out."

"THIS IS POINTLESS," he heard Shelby mutter as they tried the fifth and final window of the Sisters of History's office. It was locked up tighter than a drum and a sign in the window indicated that the society met only on the third Wednesday of the month.

"I think we've got enough for a warrant," he said as he stifled the urge to break one of the glass panes and save them all some time and trouble.

"We'll go to my place, and I'll call Jay to make the arrangements."

"What good will a warrant do? I doubt they have Chad stashed in their file cabinets."

"But I bet they have membership rosters. When we find Katherine, we find our son."

He liked saying that. Liked the way it felt on his tongue. *Our son,* he repeated as they went back to his car. *We just have to find him.*

"This is where you live?" Shelby asked not ten minutes later, when he'd turned into the small lot facing his building.

"What's the matter? Don't like the neighborhood?"

"It isn't that," she answered with a smile. "I looked at these places when I was pregnant. I thought an apartment might be easier to manage with a baby."

"It would have been," he said against her ear as they climbed the steps. "Because you would have had me, too."

His daily dose of patience dried up the moment he saw Miss Dog Expert perched at the top of the steps. She was snarling.

"It's about time, Mr. Tanner."

"Nice to see you, too, Mrs. James."

"Johns!" she fired back at him. "That dog of yours has been howling almost nonstop since right around midnight."

"Sorry," Dylan mumbled as he tried to steer Shelby around the hateful presence. "I'll take care of him."

"You'd have thought someone was breaking in down at your place, the way that animal carried on. It was almost as bad as last time."

"Down, boy," Dylan said as he caught Foolish in mid-leap. "Don't worry," he told Shelby. "He's harmless."

"Not according to your neighbor."

"My neighbor is a shriveled-up nag." He had to slap the dog's paws away at least a half-dozen more times just to get to the kitchen. "Get down!"

"Come here, puppy," Shelby said, going down on one knee to greet the dog on his own terms.

"Don't encourage him," Dylan growled, just before making the call to Jay to arrange for the warrant.

"Foolish!" he yelled, turning just in time to watch the animal tackle Shelby and plaster her against the floor. "I said *no.*" Dylan gave a sturdy yank on the dog's collar, freeing Shelby and restoring some semblance of calm.

Bracing her hand against the wall, Shelby cautiously got to her feet. He was surprised to see the spark of laughter in her light eyes. "You think he's funny?"

"He's great," she said as she patted the dog's straining head. "He's just all wired because you left him alone last night."

"No, he isn't," Dylan countered easily. "He's always like this."

"Then he's lonely. You don't pay enough attention to the poor thing."

"Poor thing?" Dylan muttered, dragging the dog to the back door and freeing him in the fenced courtyard. "I should have taken him straight to the pound that first night."

"Don't be so mean," Shelby admonished, slapping playfully at his arm as he walked in her direction. "Can I use your phone to let Rose know where I am?"

"Help yourself."

He tried not to watch her. Tried, but didn't succeed. There was just something about her that drew his attention. Part of it was looks. There was no question but that he thought she was beautiful. All that dark hair, and those big blue eyes. That small, perfect body of hers. But he knew it was more than just physical. He admired her strength. He appreciated her sharp mind, her quick intelligence. In short, he loved her.

"Really?"

The excited little edge to her voice focused his attention. He saw her scrounging around for something to write on and solved the dilemma by grabbing a grocery receipt and offering her his pen.

"Tory, I can't thank you enough." She twirled, her full skirt billowing out from her legs on the rush of air. "Tory called one of her professors and got the home telephone number of the president of the Sisters of History."

He lifted her off the ground and planted a loud kiss smack on her lips. Foolish barked wildly on the other side of the glass, while Dylan danced her through the apartment. He had a good feeling about this. And it certainly didn't hurt that she was plastered against him.

"I'll call," Dylan said as he took the paper from her hand.

In less than ten minutes, he had the woman agreeing to meet them back at the office for a full inspection of the files.

"Should we call Jay and tell him not to bother with the warrant?" Shelby asked.

"Nope. Best to cover all the bases. This broad may change her mind, and then we'll still have the warrant."

"I don't think Mrs. Pennington-Smythe is the type of woman you call a broad," Shelby warned as they headed back to the car.

She stopped short, grabbing his hand. "You left the dog outside. Won't he bother the neighbors?"

"I sure hope so," Dylan said with a sly grin. "Then maybe she'll pay more attention when someone jimmies the lock on my door."

"That's not very nice," Shelby chastened.

"She wasn't very nice to me when she watched some dirtball—"

Dylan's voice trailed off as the gears of his brain suddenly cranked into overdrive.

"What?" Shelby asked, tugging his hand.

"Let me check something with Mrs. Johns."

"While you do that, I'll let Foolish back inside."

Grudgingly Dylan handed her his keys before bounding up the stairs. He knocked furiously, knowing full well the old bat was inside.

"Yes?" she said from the opposite side of the door.

"It's me, Mrs. Johns. Dylan Tanner."

"Yes?"

"I need you to tell me something."

She opened the door and eyed him cautiously from above the rims of her thick glasses. "What is it?"

"You thought the guy who broke...uh, who was 'working' on my door was me, right?" He waited for her uncertain nod. "Why did you think that?"

"He looked like you."

Keith's voice, reciting nearly the exact same words, filtered through his brain.

"And the jacket, of course," she added.

"Jacket?"

"The one you wear. The blue one with ATF painted on the back."

Dylan treated Mrs. Johns to a loud, damp kiss and a twirl. When he placed her on the ground, he noticed that she teetered and stabbed her glasses back up her nose.

"A simple thank-you would have been sufficient," she grumbled as she stumbled back into her apartment.

Dylan found Shelby waiting at the base of the stairs. He didn't bother sharing his suspicions, not yet.

Mrs. Pennington-Smythe was waiting for them at the entrance. Her perfectly styled blue-white hair seemed impervious to the heat and humidity of the afternoon. She led the way in her sensible, midheeled leather pumps, a flaxen handbag dangling from the crook of her arm.

"I can't imagine what interest you could have in any of our members."

"Just routine," Dylan assured her. "Do you know how many Katherines you have, offhand?"

"Let me see," she said as she tapped her blunt-filed nail against her even blunter chin. "There's Katherine Morrison, of Morrison Department Stores. Katherine Jenkins—her husband's family has organized the arts festival since its inception. And Katherine Williams. Her late husband—"

"I don't care if he was the Wizard of Oz," Dylan said, interrupting her. "Get me her application."

Shelby gasped behind him. "Is it possible? Or too much of a coincidence?" she whispered.

"Katherine isn't in trouble, is she?" Mrs. Pennington-Smythe asked as she nervously unlocked the file drawer. "I recall her being a rather reserved woman."

"Is she Jay's mother?" Shelby asked as she tugged on his shirtsleeve.

"Here we are," she said, opening a folder.

Dylan grabbed the whole thing from her trembling hand and sought the information with his own eyes. He found it on page two, item seven: "Nearest Living Relative, Jay Williams, nephew."

"What does this mean?" The pleading quality of Shelby's voice only served to shove the knife deeper into his gut.

Not Jay. They were friends. There had to be some other explanation.

"Thank you for your assistance, ma'am," Dylan said to the startled woman. "I would appreciate it if you could keep this visit confidential. We wouldn't want to sully any reputations needlessly."

"Of course not," she answered.

"Whose reputation? And is this Katherine Jay's mother?"

"Aunt."

"Jay is behind all this?" she managed to choke out.

Dylan wasn't much help to her. He was having a difficult time reconciling what he had learned with the man he had known and trusted.

"I don't know, yet. We'll see when we get there."

"Get where?"

"We're going to see Katherine Williams."

Dylan didn't speak to her as they drove across town. Shelby's nerves were knotted as tightly as Dylan's white-knuckled grip on the wheel. The rage emanating from him was almost palpable. Shelby knew exactly how he was feeling. If Jay was somehow involved in all this, the betrayal Dylan was experiencing would be similar to what she had gone through when Ned announced that his only reason for associating with her was to bring some respectability to his shady business. Shelby also knew he would get through it. She'd make sure of it.

Katherine's address led them down a tree-lined drive in North Charleston. The homes were older, with fences and wide, flat lawns. Katherine's was a brick rancher with rounded shrubs and a black Taurus parked in front.

"I'll go and—"

She didn't let Dylan finish the sentence. She was out of the car and at the front door like a shot. He reached her side as she depressed the doorbell.

"Chad! Baby!" she yelled, snatching the child from the woman before she even had an opportunity to react.

"Wait."

"Back up," Dylan commanded. Then she heard him ask, "Is he okay?"

"Perfect," Shelby said through tears of absolute joy. She hugged him, smelled him, and placed kisses all over his wriggling face. "I missed you so much," she cooed.

"There has to be some sort of misunderstanding," Katherine stammered.

"Not unless you've got a good explanation for kidnapping my son," Dylan told her.

"That isn't possible!" Katherine wailed. "That little boy is in the protective custody of the federal government. We can call my nephew, Jay—"

"Enough!" Dylan thundered. Then he read her the requisite Miranda warnings. They disappeared into the house briefly, with Dylan emerging alone a few minutes later.

"Care to introduce me?" he said, in a surprisingly soft voice.

"Dylan, meet Chad," she said, putting her son in his outstretched arms.

If she hadn't already told him the truth, Dylan would have known at this instant. Her tears resumed as she looked between father and son. Chad was a near-perfect replica of the tall man tossing him in the air. Her son's squeals of delight tugged at her heart, as did the beaming smile she saw on Dylan's face.

This magical moment was intruded upon by encroaching sirens. "Did you call?"

"Yes," he said, before placing a wet kiss on Chad's exposed belly.

"What about Jay?" She reached for his arm. "Don't you want to talk to him first?"

"He'll be here," he answered casually. "Called him, too."

His calm bothered her, but the arrival of a swarm of officers prevented her from delving too deeply. She also soon realized that nothing short of a crowbar could pry Chad away from Dylan.

Dylan cradled the baby against him as he stood, swaying, in the living room of the strange house. Shelby was on the sofa, and Katherine sat motionless in a high-backed chair. Several officers lingered in the kitchen, their conversation nothing more than a hum. Chad was nearly asleep, his tiny fist filled with a wrinkled wad of Dylan's shirt.

Her only glimpse of Dylan's emotional state was the dangerous glint in his eyes. When the sound of a car door closing reached her ears, Shelby stiffened.

Katherine's expression grew even more solemn.

Carefully Dylan extracted the groggy infant and carefully handed him to Shelby.

"What are you going to do?"

"Don't know," he answered under his breath.

Jay walked in, looking angry and flustered. Dylan was there to greet him. Or, more accurately, his fist was. Katherine cried out, Shelby sucked in an audible breath, and the officers came running.

Dylan simply shook his fist, turned and claimed his family.

Epilogue

"Shelby!" he called, kicking at the dog as he balanced the three bags of groceries and tried to close the door.

"Foolish, sit."

The dog whimpered once, then skulked off into the living room and sat.

Shelby got up on tiptoe and planted a kiss on his open mouth. "Welcome back," she said sweetly.

"Da...Da...Da..." Chad sang from his high chair.

"Hi, sport," he called as he placed the heavy bags on the kitchen table.

Chad got his kiss first, Shelby noted with a dramatic frown. "I might get jealous if you keep putting him above me."

"No way," Dylan countered, pulling her into the circle of his arms and kissing her deeply and thoroughly. "You're a better kisser. Not as sloppy."

"Gee..." She sighed. "You sure know how to make a girl feel special."

"How about me?" he teased, stealing one of Chad's Cheerios, throwing it in the air and catching it in his mouth. Chad clapped. "It's very emasculating for me that Foolish hangs on your every command and I can't even get him to stand still long enough to put his leash on."

"He'd listen to you if you talked nicely to him," she said, with a taunting shake of her finger.

"I don't want to talk nicely to him. He's a traitor."

"No," she said softly, watching his eyes. "Jay was the traitor. Foolish is just a dog."

Dylan closed up and stalked into the other room. Wiping her hands on the dish towel, Shelby followed.

"Wait a minute," she implored, touching his arm.

Dylan rammed his hands in the front pockets of his jeans, his eyes distant and hard.

"It's been over two months," she began softly, her hand moving from his arm to his chest. She could feel the uneven beating of his heart beneath her fingers.

"And it is over," he insisted tightly. "Jay's admitted that he took Chad in the hopes of convincing you to testify against Nichols. He figured if he played the hero, you'd be so grateful, you'd turn on Ned without a look back."

"He was obsessed, Dylan. He lost sight of his priorities. And," she added more gently, "he'll pay for what he did."

"Not the way he should pay," Dylan countered.

"What do you want?"

"Nothing."

"Yes, you do," she said with a disgusted shrug. "You want to know how someone you trusted could betray you."

"Maybe."

"But Jay didn't know Chad was your son. He only left your medallion in the bushes so your office would be called. He didn't plan on you being involved."

"But I was involved."

"Jay didn't know that, not any more than you knew that Ned was my father when you begged me to help you to put him behind bars."

"Can't we just drop this?" he groaned.

"Not if you want to get married."

His expression darkened, and he gave her a wilting look. "Are you telling me you won't marry me now?"

"I'm telling you that I don't want to get married when you haven't come to grips with what brought us together."

Dylan raked his hand through his hair and turned his back. Foolish lifted his snout off the carpet and regarded him with disinterest.

Shelby felt as if she might explode with frustration. She glared at the steady rise and fall of his broad shoulders.

"You're right," he said, so softly that she almost missed it.

She went to him immediately, reaching around his waist and pressing her face against his back.

"Jay will be punished, and Nichols will probably trip up somewhere along the line. But none of that would matter to me if I didn't.have you and Chad in my life."

"I love you."

"I love you, too," he said as he pulled her around to place a meaningful kiss on her lips.

"I knew there was a brain beneath all that brawn," she quipped, tapping her fingertip against his chest.

"Wrong," he said, setting her on the floor. "I just don't have the guts to call my mother and tell her there won't be a wedding in Loganville this Thanksgiving."

Shelby stepped away from him, her eyes carefully shielded from his scrutiny. "Stay right there," she instructed. She raced up to the bedroom and back in record time.

With nervous fingers, she held the small velvet case out for his inspection. One dark brow arched questioningly.

"What is it?"

"Open it."

His eyes grew wide as he lifted the thick gold band from the box. "Aren't you being a bit premature?"

"No," she managed to say, despite her tight throat. "We have to get married."

"I know that. November twenty-fourth, in—"

"No," she interjected. "I mean, we *have* to get married."

"Chad's nearly a year old. I think it's a bit late to be worried about proprieties."

"Fine," she snapped. "Then I hope your mother won't mind me waltzing down the aisle...let me see—" she stopped and made a production of counting on her fingers "—six months pregnant."

She held her breath, expecting something—anything but the long silence. Finally, when she couldn't stand it any longer, Shelby peered up at him through the veil of her lashes. Then she laughed.

"I believe that expression is referred to as 'dumb-struck.'"

"Again? Really? So soon?"

"Yes, yes and yes," she answered. "I'm beginning to understand why your mother had six children. You Tanners are a prolific lot."

He kissed her then. Allaying her fears and making her feel like the luckiest woman alive.

"Do you remember that day when we were looking for Chad and we took that god-awful bike ride on the beach?"

"Sure," he answered as his hands inched down to her waist.

"You asked me what I would tell Chad about his father."

His hands stilled. "You said you had the right child with the wrong man."

"I'd like to amend that," she said as she grasped his hand and slipped the ring off the tip of his forefinger. "Read the inscription."

The right man.

HARLEQUIN®

I N T R I G U E®

**HARLEQUIN INTRIGUE AUTHOR KELSEY ROBERTS
SERVES UP A DOUBLE DOSE OF DANGER AND DESIRE
IN THE EXCITING NEW MINISERIES:**

THE ROSE TATTOO

In June we served up the first in "The Rose Tattoo" series,
#326 UNSPOKEN CONFESSIONS, which featured a tall, dark
and delectable hero and a sweet and sassy heroine.
Continuing on with the series, we're proud to present:

On the Menu for July - #330 UNLAWFULLY WEDDED

J. D. Porter—hot and spicy
Tory Conway—sinfully rich
Southern Fried Secrets—succulent and juicy

On the Menu for August - #334 UNDYING LAUGHTER

Wes Porter—subtly scrumptious
Destiny Talbott—tart and tangy
Mouth-Watering Mystery—deceptively delicious

Look for Harlequin Intrigue's response to your
hearty appetite for suspense: THE ROSE TATTOO,
where Southern specialties are served up
with a side order of suspense.

HARLEQUIN®

I N T R I G U E®

Into a world where danger lurks around
every corner, and there's a fine line between trust
and betrayal, comes a tall, dark and handsome man.

Intuition draws you to him...but instinct keeps you
away. Is he really one of those...

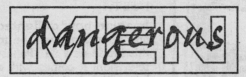

Don't miss even one of the twelve sexy but secretive
men, coming to you one per month in 1995.

In July, look for:
#329 WINTER'S EDGE
by Anne Stuart

**Take a walk on the wild side...with our
"DANGEROUS MEN"!**

ANNOUNCING THE

PRIZE SURPRISE SWEEPSTAKES!

This month's prize:

L-A-R-G-E–SCREEN PANASONIC TV!

This month, as a special surprise, we're giving away a fabulous FREE TV!

Imagine how delighted you and your family will be to own this brand-new 31" Panasonic** television! It comes with all the latest high-tech features, like a SuperFlat picture tube for a clear, crisp picture...unified remote control...closed-caption decoder...clock and sleep timer, and much more!

The facing page contains two Entry Coupons (as does every book you received this shipment). Complete and return *all* the entry coupons; **the more times you enter, the better your chances of winning the TV!**

Then keep your fingers crossed, because you'll find out by July 15, 1995 if you're the winner!

Remember: The more times you enter, the better your chances of winning!*

PTV KAL

PRIZE SURPRISE
SWEEPSTAKES

OFFICIAL ENTRY COUPON

This entry must be received by: JUNE 30, 1995
This month's winner will be notified by: JULY 15, 1995

YES, I want to win the Panasonic 31" TV! Please enter me in the drawing
and let me know if I've won!

Name_____

Address _____ Apt. _____

City   State/Prov.   Zip/Postal Code

Account #_____

Return entry with invoice in reply envelope.

© 1995 HARLEQUIN ENTERPRISES LTD.   CTV KAL

PRIZE SURPRISE
SWEEPSTAKES

OFFICIAL ENTRY COUPON

This entry must be received by: JUNE 30, 1995
This month's winner will be notified by: JULY 15, 1995

YES, I want to win the Panasonic 31" TV! Please enter me in the drawing
and let me know if I've won!

Name_____

Address _____ Apt. _____

City   State/Prov.   Zip/Postal Code

Account #_____

Return entry with invoice in reply envelope.

© 1995 HARLEQUIN ENTERPRISES LTD.   CTV KAL

OFFICIAL RULES

PRIZE SURPRISE SWEEPSTAKES 3448

NO PURCHASE OR OBLIGATION NECESSARY

Three Harlequin Reader Service 1995 shipments will contain respectively, coupons for entry into three different prize drawings, one for a Panasonic 31" wide-screen TV, another for a 5-piece Wedgwood china service for eight and the third for a Sharp ViewCam camcorder. To enter any drawing using an Entry Coupon, simply complete and mail according to directions.

There is no obligation to continue using the Reader Service to enter and be eligible for any prize drawing. You may also enter any drawing by hand printing the words "Prize Surprise," your name and address on a 3"x5" card and the name of the prize you wish that entry to be considered for (i.e., Panasonic wide-screen TV, Wedgwood china or Sharp ViewCam). Send your 3"x5" entries via first-class mail (limit: one per envelope) to: Prize Surprise Sweepstakes 3448, c/o the prize you wish that entry to be considered for, P.O. Box 1315, Buffalo, NY 14269-1315, USA or P.O. Box 610, Fort Erie, Ontario L2A 5X3, Canada.

To be eligible for the Panasonic wide-screen TV, entries must be received by 6/30/95; for the Wedgwood china, 8/30/95; and for the Sharp ViewCam, 10/30/95.

Winners will be determined in random drawings conducted under the supervision of D.L. Blair, Inc., an independent judging organization whose decisions are final, from among all eligible entries received for that drawing. Approximate prize values are as follows: Panasonic wide-screen TV ($1,800); Wedgwood china ($840) and Sharp ViewCam ($2,000). Sweepstakes open to residents of the U.S. (except Puerto Rico) and Canada, 18 years of age or older. Employees and immediate family members of Harlequin Enterprises, Ltd., D.L. Blair, Inc., their affiliates, subsidiaries and all other agencies, entities and persons connected with the use, marketing or conduct of this sweepstakes are not eligible. Odds of winning a prize are dependent upon the number of eligible entries received for that drawing. Prize drawing and winner notification for each drawing will occur no later than 15 days after deadline for entry eligibility for that drawing. Limit: one prize to an individual, family or organization. All applicable laws and regulations apply. Sweepstakes offer void wherever prohibited by law. Any litigation within the province of Quebec respecting the conduct and awarding of the prizes in this sweepstakes must be submitted to the Regies des loteries et Courses du Quebec. In order to win a prize, residents of Canada will be required to correctly answer a time-limited arithmetical skill-testing question. Value of prizes are in U.S. currency.

Winners will be obligated to sign and return an Affidavit of Eligibility within 30 days of notification. In the event of noncompliance within this time period, prize may not be awarded. If any prize or prize notification is returned as undeliverable, that prize will not be awarded. By acceptance of a prize, winner consents to use of his/her name, photograph or other likeness for purposes of advertising, trade and promotion on behalf of Harlequin Enterprises, Ltd., without further compensation, unless prohibited by law.

For the names of prizewinners (available after 12/31/95), send a self-addressed, stamped envelope to: Prize Surprise Sweepstakes 3448 Winners, P.O. Box 4200, Blair, NE 68009.

RPZ KAL